Favourite
Stories
of
COURAGEOUS
GIRLS

Hodder
Children's
Books

HODDER CHILDREN'S BOOKS
First published in Great Britain in 2019 by Hodder & Stoughton

1 3 5 7 9 10 8 6 4 2

Extracts from Enid Blyton © Hodder & Stoughton Limited
Enid Blyton®, Enid Blyton's signature, Malory Towers and St Clare's are
registered trade marks of Hodder & Stoughton Limited
Illustrations © Nan Lawson, 2019

The moral right of the authors has been asserted.

A CIP catalogue record for this book is available from the British Library.

ISBN 978 1 444 95231 5

Typeset in Caslon Twelve by Avon DataSet Ltd, Bidford-on-Avon, Warwickshire

Printed and bound in Great Britain by Clays Ltd, Elcograf S.p.A.

The paper and board used in this book are made from wood
from responsible sources.

Hodder Children's Books
An imprint of Hachette Children's Group
Part of Hodder & Stoughton
Carmelite House
50 Victoria Embankment
London, EC4Y 0DZ

An Hachette UK Company
www.hachette.co.uk
www.hachettechildrens.co.uk

CONTENTS

LITTLE WOMEN

Louisa May Alcott

Little Women is about the four March sisters – Meg, Jo, Beth and Amy – as they grow up under the loving guidance of their mother, Marmee. The girls' father is away from home, serving as a pastor in the American Civil War. The story follows the adventures and struggles of the girls, who are often joined by their neighbour Laurie.

'November is the most disagreeable *month* in the whole year,' said Margaret, standing at the window one dull afternoon, looking out at the frost-bitten garden.

'That's the reason I was born in it,' observed Jo pensively, quite unconscious of the blot on her nose.

'If something very pleasant should happen now, we should think it a delightful month,' said Beth, who took a hopeful view of everything, even November.

'I dare say; but nothing pleasant ever *does* happen in this family,' said Meg, who was out of sorts. 'We go grubbing along day after day, without a bit of change, and very little fun. We might as well be in a treadmill.'

'My patience, how blue we are!' cried Jo. 'I don't much wonder, poor dear, for you see other girls having splendid times, while you grind, grind, year in and year out. Oh, don't I wish I could manage things for you as I do for my heroines! You're pretty enough and good enough already, so I'd have some rich relation leave you a fortune unexpectedly; then you'd dash out as an heiress, scorn everyone who has slighted you, go abroad, and come home my Lady Something, in a blaze of splendour and elegance.'

'People don't have fortunes left them in that style nowadays; men have to work, and women to marry for money. It's a dreadfully unjust world,' said Meg bitterly.

'Jo and I are going to make fortunes for you all; just wait ten years, and see if we don't,' said Amy, who sat in a corner, making mud pies, as Hannah called her little clay models of birds, fruit and faces.

'Can't wait, and I'm afraid I haven't much faith in ink and dirt, though I'm grateful for your good intentions.'

Meg sighed, and turned to the frost-bitten garden again; Jo groaned, and leaned both elbows on the table in a despondent attitude, but Amy spatted away energetically; and Beth, who sat at the other window, said, smiling, 'Two pleasant things are going to happen right away: Marmee is coming down the street, and Laurie is tramping through the garden as if he had something nice to tell.'

In they both came, Mrs March with her usual question, 'Any letter from Father, girls?' and Laurie to say in his persuasive way, 'Won't some of you come for a drive? I've been working away at mathematics till my head is in a muddle, and I'm going to freshen my wits by a brisk turn. It's a dull day, but the air isn't bad, and I'm going to take Brooke home, so it will be gay inside, if it isn't out. Come, Jo, you and Beth will go, won't you?'

'Of course we will.'

'Much obliged, but I'm busy;' and Meg whisked out her work basket, for she had agreed with her mother that it was best, for her at least, not to drive often with the young gentleman.

'We three will be ready in a minute,' cried Amy, running away to wash her hands.

'Can I do anything for you, Madam Mother?' asked Laurie, leaning over Mrs March's chair, with the affectionate look and tone he always gave her.

'No, thank you, except call at the office, if you'll be so kind, dear. It's our day for a letter, and the postman hasn't been. Father is as regular as the sun, but there's some delay on the way, perhaps.'

A sharp ring interrupted her, and a minute after Hannah came in with a letter.

'It's one of them horrid telegraph things, mum,' she said, handing it as if she was afraid it would explode and do some damage.

At the word 'telegraph', Mrs March snatched it, read the two lines it contained, and dropped back into her chair as white as if the little paper had sent a bullet to her heart. Laurie dashed downstairs for water, while Meg and Hannah supported her, and Jo read aloud, in a frightened voice, 'Mrs March: Your husband is very ill. Come at once. S. Hale, Blank Hospital, Washington.'

How still the room was as they listened breathlessly, how strangely the day darkened outside, and how suddenly the whole world seemed to change, as the girls gathered about their mother, feeling as if all the happiness and support of their lives was about to be taken from them. Mrs March was herself again directly; read the message over, and stretched out her arms to her daughters, saying, in a tone they never forgot, 'I shall go at once, but it may be too late. O children, children, help me to bear it!'

For several minutes there was nothing but the sound

of sobbing in the room, mingled with broken words of comfort, tender assurances of help, and hopeful whispers that died away in tears. Poor Hannah was the first to recover, and with unconscious wisdom she set all the rest a good example; for, with her, work was the panacea for most afflictions.

'The Lord keep the dear man! I won't waste no time a cryin', but git your things ready right away, mum,' she said, heartily, as she wiped her face on her apron, gave her mistress a warm shake of the hand with her own hard one, and went away, to work like three women in one.

'She's right; there's no time for tears now. Be calm, girls, and let me think.'

They tried to be calm, poor things, as their mother sat up, looking pale, but steady, and put away her grief to think and plan for them.

'Where's Laurie?' she asked presently, when she had collected her thoughts, and decided on the first duties to be done.

'Here, ma'am. Oh, let me do something!' cried the boy, hurrying from the next room, whither he had withdrawn, feeling that their first sorrow was too sacred for even his friendly eyes to see.

'Send a telegram saying I will come at once. The next train goes early in the morning. I'll take that.'

'What else? The horses are ready; I can go anywhere, do anything,' he said, looking ready to fly to the ends of the earth.

'Leave a note at Aunt March's. Jo, give me that pen and paper.'

Tearing off the blank side of one of her newly copied pages, Jo drew the table before her mother, well knowing that money for the long, sad journey must be borrowed, and feeling as if she could do anything to add a little to the sum for her father.

'Now go, dear; but don't kill yourself driving at a desperate pace; there is no need of that.'

Mrs March's warning was evidently thrown away; for five minutes later Laurie tore by the window on his own fleet horse, riding as if for his life.

'Jo, run to the rooms, and tell Mrs King that I can't come. On the way get these things. I'll put them down; they'll be needed, and I must go prepared for nursing. Hospital stores are not always good. Beth, go and ask Mr Laurence for a couple of bottles of old wine: I'm not too proud to beg for Father; he shall have the best of everything. Amy, tell Hannah to get down the black trunk; and, Meg, come and help me find my things, for I'm half bewildered.'

Writing, thinking and directing, all at once, might well bewilder the poor lady, and Meg begged her to sit quietly in her room for a little while, and let them work. Everyone scattered like leaves before a gust of wind; and the quiet, happy household was broken up as suddenly as if the paper had been an evil spell.

Mr Laurence came hurrying back with Beth, bringing every comfort the kind old gentleman could think of for the invalid, and friendliest promises of protection for the girls during the mother's absence, which comforted her very much. There was nothing he didn't offer, from his own dressing gown to himself as escort. But that last was impossible. Mrs March would not hear of the old gentleman's undertaking the long journey; yet an expression of relief was visible when he spoke of it, for anxiety ill fits one for travelling. He saw the look, knit his heavy eyebrows, rubbed his hands and marched abruptly away, saying he'd be back directly. No one had time to think of him again till, as Meg ran through the entry, with a pair of rubbers in one hand and a cup of tea in the other, she came suddenly upon Mr Brooke.

'I'm very sorry to hear of this, Miss March,' he said in the kind, quiet tone which sounded very pleasantly to her perturbed spirit. 'I came to offer myself as escort to your mother. Mr Laurence has commissions for me in Washington, and it will give me real satisfaction to be of service to her there.'

Down dropped the rubbers, and the tea was very near

following, as Meg put out her hand, with a face so full of gratitude, that Mr Brooke would have felt repaid for a much greater sacrifice than the trifling one of time and comfort which he was about to make.

'How kind you all are! Mother will accept, I'm sure; and it will be such a relief to know that she has someone to take care of her. Thank you very, very much!'

Meg spoke earnestly, and forgot herself entirely till something in the brown eyes looking down at her made her remember the cooling tea, and lead the way into the parlour, saying she would call her mother.

Everything was arranged by the time Laurie returned with a note from Aunt March, enclosing the desired sum, and a few lines repeating what she had often said before – that she had always told them it was absurd for March to go into the army, always predicted that no good would come of it, and she hoped they would take her advice next time. Mrs March put the note in the fire, the money in her purse, and went on with her preparations, with her lips folded tightly, in a way which Jo would have understood if she had been there.

The short afternoon wore away; all the other errands were done, and Meg and her mother busy at some necessary needlework, while Beth and Amy got tea, and Hannah finished her ironing with what she called a 'slap and a bang', but still Jo did not come.

They began to get anxious; and Laurie went off to find her, for no one ever knew what freak Jo might take into her head. He missed her, however, and she came walking in with a very queer expression of countenance, for there was a mixture of fun and fear, satisfaction and regret in it, which puzzled the family as much as did the roll of bills she laid before her mother, saying, with a little choke in her voice, 'That's my contribution towards making Father comfortable and bringing him home!'

'My dear, where did you get it? Twenty-five dollars! Jo, I hope you haven't done anything rash?'

'No, it's mine honestly; I didn't beg, borrow, or steal it. I earned it; and I don't think you'll blame me, for I only sold what was my own.'

As she spoke, Jo took off her bonnet, and a general outcry arose, for all her abundant hair was cut short.

'Your hair! Your beautiful hair!'

'O Jo, how could you? Your one beauty.'

'My dear girl, there was no need of this.'

'She doesn't look like my Jo any more, but I love her dearly for it!'

As everyone exclaimed, and Beth hugged the cropped head tenderly, Jo assumed an indifferent air, which did not deceive anyone a particle, and said, rumpling up the brown bush, and trying to look as if she liked it, 'It doesn't affect the fate of the nation, so don't wail, Beth. It will be good for my vanity; I was getting too proud of my wig. It will do my brains good to have that mop taken off; my head feels deliciously light and cool, and the barber said I could soon have a curly crop, which will be boyish, becoming and easy to keep in order. I'm satisfied; so please take the money, and let's have supper.'

'Tell me all about it, Jo. *I* am not quite satisfied, but I can't blame you, for I know how willingly you sacrificed your vanity, as you call it, to your love. But, my dear, it was not necessary, and I'm afraid you will regret it, one of these days,' said Mrs March.

'No, I won't!' returned Jo stoutly, feeling much relieved that her prank was not entirely condemned.

'What made you do it?' asked Amy, who would as soon have thought of cutting off her head as her pretty hair.

'Well, I was wild to do something for Father,' replied Jo, as they gathered about the table, for healthy young people can eat even in the midst of trouble. 'I hate to borrow as much as Mother does, and I knew Aunt March would croak; she always does, if you ask for a ninepence. Meg gave all her quarterly salary toward the rent, and I only got some clothes with mine, so I felt wicked, and was bound to have some money, if

I sold the nose off my face to get it.'

'You needn't feel wicked, my child: you had no winter things, and got the simplest with your own hard earnings,' said Mrs March, with a look that warmed Jo's heart.

'I hadn't the least idea of selling my hair at first, but as I went along I kept thinking what I could do, and feeling as if I'd like to dive into some of the rich stores and help myself. In a barber's window I saw tails of hair with the prices marked; and one black tail, not so thick as mine, was forty dollars. It came over me all of a sudden that I had one thing to make money out of, and without stopping to think, I walked in, asked if they bought hair, and what they would give for mine.'

'I don't see how you dared to do it,' said Beth, in a tone of awe.

'Oh, he was a little man who looked as if he merely lived to oil his hair. He rather stared, at first, as if he wasn't used to having girls bounce into his shop and ask him to buy their hair. He said he didn't care about mine, it wasn't the fashionable colour, and he never paid much for it in the first place; the work put into it made it dear, and so on. It was getting late, and I was afraid, if it wasn't done right away, that I shouldn't have it done at all, and you know when I start to do a thing, I hate to give it up; so I begged him to take it, and told him why I was in such a hurry. It was silly, I dare say, but it changed his mind, for I got rather excited, and told the story in my topsy-turvy way, and his wife heard, and said so kindly, '"Take it, Thomas, and oblige the young lady; I'd do as much for our Jimmy any day if I had a spire of hair worth selling."'

'Who was Jimmy?' asked Amy, who liked to have things explained as they went along.

'Her son, she said, who was in the army. How friendly such things make strangers feel, don't they? She talked away all the time the man clipped, and diverted my mind nicely.'

'Didn't you feel dreadfully when the first cut came?' asked Meg, with a shiver.

'I took a last look at my hair while the man got his things, and that was the end of it. I never snivel over trifles like that; I will confess, though, I felt queer when I saw the dear old hair laid out on the table, and felt only the short, rough ends on my head. It almost seemed as if I'd an arm or a leg off. The woman saw me look at it, and picked out a long lock for me to keep. I'll give it to you, Marmee, just to remember past glories by; for a crop is so comfortable I don't think I shall ever have a mane again.'

Mrs March folded the wavy, chestnut lock, and laid it away with a short grey one in her desk. She only said

'Thank you, deary,' but something in her face made the girls change the subject, and talk as cheerfully as they could about Mr Brooke's kindness, the prospect of a fine day tomorrow, and the happy times they would have when Father came home to be nursed.

No one wanted to go to bed, when, at ten o'clock, Mrs March put by the last finished job, and said, 'Come, girls.' Beth went to the piano and played their father's favourite hymn; all began bravely, but broke down one by one, till Beth was left alone, singing with all her heart, for to her music was always a sweet consoler.

'Go to bed and don't talk, for we must be up early, and shall need all the sleep we can get. Goodnight, my darlings,' said Mrs March, as the hymn ended, for no one cared to try another.

They kissed her quietly, and went to bed as silently as if the dear invalid lay in the next room. Beth and Amy soon fell asleep in spite of the great trouble, but Meg lay awake, thinking the most serious thoughts she had ever known in her short life. Jo lay motionless, and her sister fancied that she was asleep, till a stifled sob made her exclaim, as she touched a wet cheek –

'Jo, dear, what is it? Are you crying about Father?'

'No, not now.'

'What then?'

'My – my hair!' burst out poor Jo, trying vainly to smother her emotion in the pillow.

It did not sound at all comical to Meg, who kissed and caressed the afflicted heroine in the tenderest manner.

'I'm not sorry,' protested Jo, with a choke. 'I'd do it again tomorrow, if I could. It's only the vain, selfish part of me that goes and cries in this silly way. Don't tell anyone, it's all over now. I thought you were asleep, so I just made a little private moan for my one beauty . . .'

The WONDERFUL WIZARD of OZ

L. Frank Baum

Dorothy's adventure begins when she and her little dog, Toto, are swept away in their house by a cyclone. The house lands in strange, magical land called Oz – right on top of the Wicked Witch of the East! The Good Witch thanks Dorothy for killing her enemy, and gives Dorothy a magical kiss on the forehead. Dorothy wants to go home, so the Good Witch tells her that she must travel along the Yellow Brick Road to the Emerald City. That's where the powerful Wizard of Oz lives, and Dorothy can ask for his help. Dorothy and Toto bravely set off, and along the way meet a Scarecrow, who joins them because he wants to ask the Wizard for a brain of his own, and a Tin Woodman, who joins them because he wants to ask the Wizard for a heart.

All this time Dorothy and her companions had been walking through the thick woods. The road was still paved with yellow brick, but these were much covered by dried branches and dead leaves from the trees, and the walking was not at all good.

There were few birds in this part of the forest, for birds love the open country where there is plenty of sunshine; but now and then there came a deep growl from some wild animal hidden among the trees. These sounds made the little girl's heart beat fast, for she did not know what made them; but Toto knew, and he walked close to Dorothy's side, and did not even bark in return.

'How long will it be,' the child asked of the Tin Woodman, 'before we are out of the forest?'

'I cannot tell,' was the answer, 'for I have never been to the Emerald City. But my father went there once, when I was a boy, and he said it was a long journey through a dangerous country, although nearer to the city where Oz dwells the country is beautiful. But I am not afraid so long as I have my oilcan, and nothing can hurt the Scarecrow, while you bear upon your forehead the mark of the good Witch's kiss, and that will protect you from harm.'

'But Toto!' said the girl, anxiously; 'what will protect him?'

'We must protect him ourselves, if he is in danger,' replied the Tin Woodman.

Just as he spoke there came from the forest a terrible

roar, and the next moment a great Lion bounded into the road. With one blow of his paw he sent the Scarecrow spinning over and over to the edge of the road, and then he struck at the Tin Woodman with his sharp claws. But, to the Lion's surprise, he could make no impression on the tin, although the Woodman fell over in the road and lay still.

Little Toto, now that he had an enemy to face, ran barking toward the Lion, and the great beast had opened his mouth to bite the dog, when Dorothy, fearing Toto would be killed, and heedless of danger, rushed forward and slapped the Lion upon his nose as hard as she could, while she cried out, 'Don't you dare to bite Toto! You ought to be ashamed of yourself, a big beast like you, to bite a poor little dog!'

'I didn't bite him,' said the Lion, as he rubbed his nose with his paw where Dorothy had hit it.

'No, but you tried to,' she retorted. 'You are nothing but a big coward.'

'I know it,' said the Lion, hanging his head in shame; 'I've always known it. But how can I help it?'

'I don't know, I'm sure. To think of your striking a stuffed man, like the poor Scarecrow!'

'Is he stuffed?' asked the Lion, in surprise, as he watched her pick up the Scarecrow and set him upon his feet, while she patted him into shape again.

'Of course he's stuffed,' replied Dorothy, who was still angry.

'That's why he went over so easily,' remarked the Lion. 'It astonished me to see him whirl around so. Is the other one stuffed, also?'

'No,' said Dorothy, 'he's made of tin.' And she helped the Woodman up again.

'That's why he nearly blunted my claws,' said the Lion. 'When they scratched against the tin it made a cold shiver run down my back. What is that little animal you are so tender of?'

'He is my dog, Toto,' answered Dorothy.

'Is he made of tin, or stuffed?' asked the Lion.

'Neither. He's a – a – a meat dog,' said the girl.

'Oh. He's a curious animal, and seems remarkably small, now that I look at him. No one would think of biting such a little thing except a coward like me,' continued the Lion sadly.

'What makes you a coward?' asked Dorothy, looking at the great beast in wonder, for he was as big as a small horse.

'It's a mystery,' replied the Lion. 'I suppose I was born that way. All the other animals in the forest naturally expect me to be brave, for the Lion is everywhere thought to be the King of Beasts. I learned that if I roared very loudly every living thing was frightened and got out of my way. Whenever I've met a man I've been awfully scared; but I just roared at him, and he has always run away as fast as he could go. If the elephants and the tigers and the bears had ever tried to fight me, I should have run myself – I'm such a coward; but just as soon as they hear me roar they all try to get away from me, and of course I let them go.'

'But that isn't right. The King of Beasts shouldn't be a coward,' said the Scarecrow.

'I know it,' returned the Lion, wiping a tear from his eye with the tip of his tail; 'it is my great sorrow, and makes my life very unhappy. But whenever there is danger my heart begins to beat fast.'

'Perhaps you have heart disease,' said the Tin Woodman.

'It may be,' said the Lion.

'If you have,' continued the Tin Woodman, 'you ought to be glad, for it proves you have a heart. For my part, I have no heart; so I cannot have heart disease.'

'Perhaps,' said the Lion, thoughtfully, 'if I had no heart I should not be a coward.'

'Have you brains?' asked the Scarecrow.

'I suppose so. I've never looked to see,' replied the Lion.

'I am going to the great Oz to ask him to give me

23

some,' remarked the Scarecrow, 'for my head is stuffed with straw.'

'And I am going to ask him to give me a heart,' said the Woodman.

'And I am going to ask him to send Toto and me back to Kansas,' added Dorothy.

'Do you think Oz could give me courage?' asked the cowardly Lion.

'Just as easily as he could give me brains,' said the Scarecrow.

'Or give me a heart,' said the Tin Woodman.

'Or send me back to Kansas,' said Dorothy.

'Then, if you don't mind, I'll go with you,' said the Lion, 'for my life is simply unbearable without a bit of courage.'

'You will be very welcome,' answered Dorothy, 'for you will help to keep away the other wild beasts. It seems to me they must be more cowardly than you are if they allow you to scare them so easily.'

'They really are,' said the Lion; 'but that doesn't make me any braver, and as long as I know myself to be a coward I shall be unhappy.'

So once more the little company set off upon the journey, the Lion walking with stately strides at Dorothy's side. Toto did not approve this new comrade at first, for he could not forget how nearly he had been crushed between the Lion's great jaws; but after a time he became more at ease, and presently Toto and the Cowardly Lion had grown to be good friends.

The SNOW QUEEN

Hans Christian Andersen

The Snow Queen *is a fairy tale about a little boy called Kay and a little girl called Gerda, who love each other like brother and sister. A long time ago, a wicked sprite made a magic mirror that had the power to make everything good seem mean and ugly. When he and his sprite friends were playing with the mirror one day they accidentally dropped it; it fell to earth and smashed into a million little pieces. If a human gets a piece of the magic mirror in their eye, it makes everything look bad, and a piece in the heart will make that heart turn as cold as ice. Unfortunately Kay gets a piece in his eye and another in his heart. Soon afterwards he sees the beautiful Snow Queen, who puts him in her sled and takes him away to her palace, where his heart grows colder and colder until he forgets his grandmother, his home and even Gerda.*

Gerda, however, does not forget Kay, and sets out to rescue him from wherever he might be. After many trials, she is kidnapped by a gang of robbers. There is a little girl robber in the gang who asks the others not to kill Gerda because she wants to keep her as a plaything. She asks Gerda to tell her about Kay and her adventure so far.

Then Gerda repeated her story over again, while the wood pigeons in the cage over her cooed, and the other pigeons slept. The little robber girl put one arm across Gerda's neck, and held the knife in the other, and was soon fast asleep and snoring. But Gerda could not close her eyes at all; she knew not whether she was to live or to die. The robbers sat round the fire, singing and drinking. It was a terrible sight for a little girl to witness.

Then the wood pigeons said, 'Coo, coo, we have seen little Kay. A white fowl carried his sledge, and he sat in the carriage of the Snow Queen, which drove through the wood while we were lying in our nest. She blew upon us, and all the young ones died, excepting us two. Coo, coo.'

'What are you saying up there?' cried Gerda. 'Where was the Snow Queen going? Do you know anything about it?'

'She was most likely travelling to Lapland, where there is always snow and ice. Ask the reindeer that is fastened up there with a rope.'

'Yes, there is always snow and ice,' said the reindeer,

'and it is a glorious place; you can leap and run about freely on the sparkling icy plains. The Snow Queen has her summer tent there, but her strong castle is at the North Pole, on an island called Spitzbergen.'

'O Kay, little Kay!' sighed Gerda.

'Lie still,' said the robber girl, 'or you shall feel my knife.'

In the morning Gerda told her all that the wood pigeons had said, and the little robber girl looked quite serious, and nodded her head and said, 'That is all talk, that is all talk. Do you know where Lapland is?' she asked the reindeer.

'Who should know better than I do?' said the animal, while his eyes sparkled. 'I was born and brought up there and used to run about the snow-covered plains.'

'Now listen,' said the robber girl; 'all our men are gone away; only Mother is here, and here she will stay; but at noon she always drinks out of a great bottle, and afterwards sleeps for a little while; and then I'll do something for you.' She jumped out of bed, clasped her mother round the neck, and pulled her by the beard, crying, 'My own little nanny goat, good morning!' And her mother pinched her nose till it was quite red; yet she did it all for love.

When the mother had gone to sleep the little robber maiden went to the reindeer and said, 'I should like very much to tickle your neck a few times more with my knife, for it makes you look so funny, but never mind – I will untie your cord and set you free, so that you may run away to Lapland; but you must make good use of your legs and carry this little maiden to the castle of the Snow Queen, where her playfellow is. You have heard what she told me, for she spoke loud enough, and you were listening.'

The reindeer jumped for joy, and the little robber girl lifted Gerda on his back and had the forethought to tie her on and even to give her her own little cushion to sit upon.

'Here are your fur boots for you,' said she, 'for it will be very cold; but I must keep the muff, it is so pretty. However, you shall not be frozen for the want of it; here are my mother's large warm mittens; they will reach up to your elbows. Let me put them on. There, now your hands look just like my mother's.'

But Gerda wept for joy.

'I don't like to see you fret,' said the little robber girl. 'You ought to look quite happy now. And here are two loaves and a ham, so that you need not starve.'

These were fastened upon the reindeer, and then the little robber maiden opened the door, coaxed in all the great dogs, cut the string with which the reindeer was fastened with her sharp knife, and said, 'Now run, but mind you take good care of the little girl.' And Gerda stretched out her hand, with the great mitten on it, towards the little robber girl and said, 'Farewell,' and away flew the reindeer over stumps and stones, through the great forest, over marshes and plains, as quickly as he could. The wolves howled and the ravens screamed, while up in the sky quivered red lights like flames of fire. 'There are my old northern lights,' said the reindeer; 'see how they flash!' And he ran on day and night still faster and faster, but the loaves and the ham were all eaten by the time they reached Lapland.

They stopped at a little hut; it was very mean-looking. The roof sloped nearly down to the ground, and the door was so low that the family had to creep in on their hands and knees when they went in and out. There was no one at home but an old Lapland woman who was dressing fish by the light of a train oil lamp.

The reindeer told her all about Gerda's story after having first told his own, which seemed to him the most important. But Gerda was so pinched with the cold that she could not speak.

'Oh, you poor things,' said the Lapland woman, 'you have a long way to go yet. You must travel more than a hundred miles further, to Finland. The Snow Queen lives there now, and she burns Bengal lights every evening. I will write a few words on a dried stockfish, for I have no paper, and you can take it from me to the Finland woman who lives there. She can give you better information than I can.'

So when Gerda was warmed and had taken something to eat and drink, the woman wrote a few words on the dried fish and told Gerda to take great care of it. Then she tied her again on the back of the reindeer, and he sprang high into the air and set off at full speed. Flash, flash, went the beautiful blue northern lights the whole night long.

And at length they reached Finland and knocked at the chimney of the Finland woman's hut, for it had no door above the ground. They crept in, but it was so terribly hot inside that the woman wore scarcely any clothes. She was small and very dirty-looking. She loosened little Gerda's dress and took off the fur boots and the mittens, or Gerda would have been unable to bear the heat; and then she placed a piece of ice on the reindeer's head and read what was written on the dried fish. After she had read it three times she knew it by heart, so she popped the fish into the soup saucepan, as she knew it was good to eat, and she never wasted anything.

The reindeer told his own story first and then little Gerda's, and the Finlander twinkled with her clever eyes, but said nothing.

'You are so clever,' said the reindeer; 'I know you can tie all the winds of the world with a piece of twine. If a sailor unties one knot, he has a fair wind; when he unties the second, it blows hard; but if the third and fourth are loosened, then comes a storm which will root up whole forests. Cannot you give this little maiden something which will make her as strong as twelve men, to overcome the Snow Queen?'

'The power of twelve men!' said the Finland woman. 'That would be of very little use.' But she went to a shelf and took down and unrolled a large skin on which were inscribed wonderful characters, and she read till the perspiration ran down from her forehead.

But the reindeer begged so hard for little Gerda, and Gerda looked at the Finland woman with such tender, tearful eyes, that her own eyes began to twinkle again. She drew the reindeer into a corner and whispered to him while she laid a fresh piece of ice on his head, 'Little Kay is really with the Snow Queen, but he finds everything there so much to his taste and his liking that he believes it is the finest place in the world; and this is because he has a piece of broken glass in his heart and a little splinter of glass in his eye. These must be taken out, or he will never be a human being again, and the Snow Queen will retain her power over him.'

'But can you not give little Gerda something to help her to conquer this power?'

'I can give her no greater power than she has already,' said the woman; 'don't you see how strong that is? How men and animals are obliged to serve her, and how well she has got through the world, barefooted as she is? She cannot receive any power from me greater than she now has, which consists in her own purity and innocence of heart. If she cannot herself obtain access to the Snow Queen and remove the glass fragments from little Kay, we can do nothing to help her. Two miles from here the Snow Queen's garden begins. You can carry the little girl so far, and set her down by the large bush which stands in the snow, covered with red berries. Do not stay gossiping, but come back here as quickly as you can.' Then the Finland woman lifted little Gerda upon the reindeer, and he ran away with her as quickly as he could.

'Oh, I have forgotten my boots and my mittens,' cried little Gerda, as soon as she felt the cutting cold; but the reindeer dared not stop, so he ran on till he reached the bush with the red berries. Here he set Gerda down, and he kissed her, and the great bright tears trickled over the animal's cheeks; then he left her and ran back as fast as he could.

There stood poor Gerda, without shoes, without

gloves, in the midst of cold, dreary, ice-bound Finland. She ran forward as quickly as she could, when a whole regiment of snowflakes came round her. They did not, however, fall from the sky, which was quite clear and glittered with the northern lights. The snowflakes ran along the ground, and the nearer they came to her the larger they appeared. Gerda remembered how large and beautiful they looked through the burning glass. But these were really larger and much more terrible, for they were alive and were the guards of the Snow Queen and had the strangest shapes. Some were like great porcupines, others like twisted serpents with their heads stretching out, and some few were like little fat bears with their hair bristled; but all were dazzlingly white, and all were living snowflakes.

Little Gerda repeated the Lord's Prayer, and the cold was so great that she could see her own breath come out of her mouth like steam, as she uttered the words. The steam appeared to increase as she continued her prayer, till it took the shape of little angels, who grew larger the moment they touched the earth. They all wore helmets on their heads and carried spears and shields. Their number continued to increase more and more, and by the time Gerda had finished her prayers a whole legion stood round her. They thrust their spears into the terrible snowflakes so that they shivered into a hundred pieces, and little Gerda could go forward with courage and safety. The angels stroked her hands and feet, so that she felt the cold less as she hastened on to the Snow Queen's castle.

But now we must see what Kay is doing. In truth he thought not of little Gerda, and least of all that she could be standing at the front of the palace.

The walls of the palace were formed of drifted snow, and the windows and doors of cutting winds. There were more than a hundred rooms in it, all as if they had been formed of snow blown together. The largest of them extended for several miles. They were all lit up by the vivid light of the aurora, and were so large and empty, so icy cold and glittering!

There were no amusements here; not even a little bear's ball, when the storm might have been the music, and the bears could have danced on their hind legs and shown their good manners. There were no pleasant games of snapdragon, or touch, nor even a gossip over the tea table for the young-lady foxes. Empty, vast and cold were the halls of the Snow Queen.

The flickering flames of the northern lights could be plainly seen, whether they rose high or low in the heavens, from every part of the castle. In the midst of this empty, endless hall of snow was a frozen lake, broken on its surface into a thousand forms; each piece resembled another, because each was in itself perfect as a work of art, and in the centre of this lake sat the Snow Queen when she was at home. She called the lake 'The Mirror of Reason', and said that it was the best, and indeed the only one, in the world.

Little Kay was quite blue with cold – indeed, almost black – but he did not feel it; for the Snow Queen had kissed away the icy shiverings, and his heart was already a lump of ice. He dragged some sharp, flat pieces of ice to and fro and placed them together in all kinds of positions, as if he wished to make something out of them – just as we try to form various figures with little tablets of wood, which we call a 'Chinese puzzle'. Kay's figures were very artistic; it was the icy game of reason at which he played, and in his eyes the figures were very remarkable and of the highest importance; this opinion was owing to the splinter of glass still sticking in his eye. He composed many complete figures, forming different words, but there was one word he never could manage to form, although he wished it very much. It was the word 'Eternity'.

The Snow Queen had said to him, 'When you can find out this, you shall be your own master, and I will give you the whole world and a new pair of skates.' But he could not accomplish it.

'Now I must hasten away to warmer countries,' said the Snow Queen. 'I will go and look into the black craters of the tops of the burning mountains, Etna and Vesuvius, as they are called. I shall make them look white, which will be good for them and for the lemons and the grapes.' And away flew the Snow Queen, leaving little Kay quite alone in the great hall which was so many miles in length. He sat and looked at his pieces of ice and was thinking so deeply and sat so still that anyone might have supposed he was frozen.

Just at this moment it happened that little Gerda came through the great door of the castle. Cutting winds were raging around her, but she offered up a prayer, and the winds sank down as if they were going to sleep. On she went till she came to the large, empty hall and caught sight of Kay. She knew him directly; she flew to him and threw her arms around his neck and held him fast while she exclaimed, 'Kay, dear little Kay, I have found you at last!'

But he sat quite still, stiff and cold.

Then little Gerda wept hot tears, which fell on his breast, and penetrated into his heart, and thawed the lump of ice, and washed away the little piece of glass which had stuck there. Then he looked at her, and she sang:

'Roses bloom and fade away,

But we the Christ Child see alway.'

Then Kay burst into tears. He wept so that the splinter of glass swam out of his eye. Then he recognised Gerda and said joyfully, 'Gerda, dear little Gerda, where have you been all this time, and where have I been?' And he looked all around him and said, 'How cold it is, and how large and empty it all looks,' and he clung to Gerda, and she laughed and wept for joy.

It was so pleasing to see them that even the pieces of ice danced, and when they were tired and went to lie down they formed themselves into the letters of the word which the Snow Queen had said he must find out before he could be his own master and have the whole world and a pair of new skates.

Gerda kissed his cheeks, and they became blooming; and she kissed his eyes till they shone like her own; she kissed his hands and feet, and he became quite healthy and cheerful. The Snow Queen might come home now when she pleased, for there stood his certainty of freedom, in the word she wanted, written in shining letters of ice.

Then they took each other by the hand and went forth from the great palace of ice.

The
RAILWAY CHILDREN

E. Nesbit

When their father is falsely accused of being a spy and is sent to prison, Roberta (Bobbie), Phyllis and Peter have to move from London to a small cottage in the Yorkshire countryside. The cottage is called Three Chimneys and is next to a railway line. Even though they are now poor and miss their father, the children find new ways to have fun and adventures, and make friends with the train drivers, workmen and some of the passengers that they see travelling on the trains every day. Bobbie is kind-hearted and always coming up with ideas to help her mother and younger siblings – and maybe even bring their father home.

They had seen the blossom on the trees in the spring, and they knew where to look for wild cherries now that cherry time was here. The trees grew all up and along the rocky face of the cliff out of which the mouth of the tunnel opened. There were all sorts of trees there, birches and beeches and baby oaks and hazels, and among them the cherry blossom had shone like snow and silver.

The mouth of the tunnel was some way from Three Chimneys, so Mother let them take their lunch with them in a basket. And the basket would do to bring the cherries back in if they found any. She also lent them her silver watch so that they should not be late for tea. Peter's Waterbury had taken it into its head not to go since the day when Peter dropped it into the water butt. And they started. When they got to the top of the cutting, they leant over the fence and looked down to where the railway lines lay at the bottom of what, as Phyllis said, was exactly like a mountain gorge.

'If it wasn't for the railway at the bottom, it would be as though the foot of man had never been there, wouldn't it?'

The sides of the cutting were of grey stone, very roughly hewn. Indeed, the top part of the cutting had been a little natural glen that had been cut deeper to bring it down to the level of the tunnel's mouth. Among the rocks, grass and flowers grew, and seeds dropped by birds in the crannies of the stone had taken root and grown into bushes and trees that overhung the cutting. Near the tunnel was a flight of steps leading down to the line – just wooden bars roughly fixed into the earth – a very steep and narrow way, more like a ladder than a stair.

'We'd better get down,' said Peter; 'I'm sure the cherries would be quite easy to get at from the side of the steps. You remember it was there we picked the cherry blossoms that we put on the rabbit's grave.'

So they went along the fence towards the little swing gate that is at the top of these steps. And they were almost at the gate when Bobbie said, 'Hush. Stop! What's that?'

'That' was a very odd noise indeed – a soft noise, but quite plainly to be heard through the sound of the wind in tree branches, and the hum and whir of the telegraph wires. It was a sort of rustling, whispering sound. As they listened it stopped, and then it began again.

And this time it did not stop, but it grew louder and more rustling and rumbling.

'Look' – cried Peter, suddenly – 'the tree over there!'

The tree he pointed at was one of those that have rough grey leaves and white flowers. The berries, when they come, are bright scarlet, but if you pick them, they disappoint you by turning black before you get them home. And, as Peter pointed, the tree was moving – not just the way trees ought to move when the wind blows through them, but all in one piece, as though it were a live creature and were walking down the side of the cutting.

'It's moving!' cried Bobbie. 'Oh, look! and so are the others. It's like the woods in *Macbeth*.'

'It's magic,' said Phyllis, breathlessly. 'I always knew this railway was enchanted.'

It really did seem a little like magic. For all the trees for about twenty yards of the opposite bank seemed to be slowly walking down towards the railway line, the tree with the grey leaves bringing up the rear like some old shepherd driving a flock of green sheep.

'What is it? Oh, what is it?' said Phyllis; 'it's much too magic for me. I don't like it. Let's go home.'

But Bobbie and Peter clung fast to the rail and watched breathlessly. And Phyllis made no movement towards going home by herself.

The trees moved on and on. Some stones and loose earth fell down and rattled on the railway metals far below.

'It's ALL coming down,' Peter tried to say, but he found there was hardly any voice to say it with. And, indeed, just as he spoke, the great rock, on the top of which the walking trees were, leant slowly forward. The trees, ceasing to walk, stood still and shivered. Leaning with the rock, they seemed to hesitate a moment, and then rock and trees and grass and bushes, with a rushing sound, slipped right away from the face of the cutting and fell on the line with a blundering crash that could have been heard half a mile off. A cloud of dust rose up.

'Oh,' said Peter, in awestruck tones, 'isn't it exactly like when coals come in? – if there wasn't any roof to the cellar and you could see down.'

'Look what a great mound it's made!' said Bobbie.

'Yes,' said Peter, slowly. He was still leaning on the fence. 'Yes,' he said again, still more slowly.

Then he stood upright.

'The 11.29 down hasn't gone by yet. We must let them know at the station, or there'll be a most frightful accident.'

'Let's run,' said Bobbie, and began.

But Peter cried, 'Come back!' and looked at Mother's watch. He was very prompt and businesslike, and his face looked whiter than they had ever seen it.

'No time,' he said; 'it's two miles away, and it's past eleven.'

'Couldn't we,' suggested Phyllis, breathlessly, 'couldn't we climb up a telegraph post and do something to the wires?'

'We don't know how,' said Peter.

'They do it in war,' said Phyllis; 'I know I've heard of it.'

'They only CUT them, silly,' said Peter, 'and that doesn't do any good. And we couldn't cut them even if we got up, and we couldn't get up. If we had anything red, we could get down on the line and wave it.'

'But the train wouldn't see us till it got round the corner, and then it could see the mound just as well as us,' said Phyllis; 'better, because it's much bigger than us.'

'If we only had something red,' Peter repeated, 'we could go round the corner and wave to the train.'

'We might wave, anyway.'

'They'd only think it was just US, as usual. We've waved so often before. Anyway, let's get down.'

They got down the steep stairs. Bobbie was pale and shivering. Peter's face looked thinner than usual. Phyllis was red-faced and damp with anxiety.

'Oh, how hot I am!' she said; 'and I thought it was going to be cold; I wish we hadn't put on our' – she stopped short, and then ended in quite a different tone – 'our flannel petticoats.'

Bobbie turned at the bottom of the stairs.

'Oh, yes,' she cried; 'THEY'RE red! Let's take them off.'

They did, and with the petticoats rolled up under their arms, ran along the railway, skirting the newly fallen mound of stones and rock and earth, and bent, crushed, twisted trees. They ran at their best pace. Peter led, but the girls were not far behind. They reached the corner that hid the mound from the straight line of railway that ran half a mile without curve or corner.

'Now,' said Peter, taking hold of the largest flannel petticoat.

'You're not' – Phyllis faltered – 'you're not going to TEAR them?'

'Shut up,' said Peter, with brief sternness.

'Oh, yes,' said Bobbie, 'tear them into little bits if you like. Don't you see, Phil, if we can't stop the train, there'll be a real live accident, with people KILLED. Oh, horrible! Here, Peter, you'll never tear it through the band!'

She took the red flannel petticoat from him and tore it off an inch from the band. Then she tore the other in the same way.

'There!' said Peter, tearing in his turn. He divided each petticoat into three pieces. 'Now, we've got six flags.' He looked at the watch again. 'And we've got seven minutes. We must have flagstaffs.'

The knives given to boys are, for some odd reason, seldom of the kind of steel that keeps sharp. The young saplings had to be broken off. Two came up by the roots. The leaves were stripped from them.

'We must cut holes in the flags, and run the sticks through the holes,' said Peter. And the holes were cut. The knife was sharp enough to cut flannel with. Two of the flags were set up in heaps of loose stones between the sleepers of the down line. Then Phyllis and Roberta took each a flag, and stood ready to wave it as soon as the train came in sight.

'I shall have the other two myself,' said Peter, 'because it was my idea to wave something red.'

'They're our petticoats, though,' Phyllis was beginning, but Bobbie interrupted.

'Oh, what does it matter who waves what, if we can only save the train?'

Perhaps Peter had not rightly calculated the number of minutes it would take the 11.29 to get from the station to the place where they were, or perhaps the train was late. Anyway, it seemed a very long time that they waited.

Phyllis grew impatient. 'I expect the watch is wrong, and the train's gone by,' said she.

Peter relaxed the heroic attitude he had chosen to show off his two flags. And Bobbie began to feel sick with suspense.

It seemed to her that they had been standing there for hours and hours, holding those silly little red flannel flags that no one would ever notice. The train wouldn't care. It would go rushing by them and tear round the corner and go crashing into that awful mound. And everyone would be killed. Her hands grew very cold and trembled so that she could hardly hold the flag. And then came the distant rumble and hum of the metals, and a puff of white steam showed far away along the stretch of line.

'Stand firm,' said Peter, 'and wave like mad! When it gets to that big furze bush step back, but go on waving! Don't stand ON the line, Bobbie!'

The train came rattling along very, very fast.

'They don't see us! They won't see us! It's all no good!' cried Bobbie.

The two little flags on the line swayed as the nearing train shook and loosened the heaps of loose stones that held them up. One of them slowly leant over and fell on the line. Bobbie jumped forward and caught it up, and waved it; her hands did not tremble now.

It seemed that the train came on as fast as ever. It was very near now.

'Keep off the line, you silly cuckoo!' said Peter, fiercely.

'It's no good,' Bobbie said again.

'Stand back!' cried Peter, suddenly, and he dragged Phyllis back by the arm.

But Bobbie cried, 'Not yet, not yet!' and waved her two flags right over the line. The front of the engine looked black and enormous. Its voice was loud and harsh.

'Oh, stop, stop, stop!' cried Bobbie. No one heard her. At least Peter and Phyllis didn't, for the oncoming rush of the train covered the sound of her voice with a mountain of sound. But afterwards she used to wonder whether the engine itself had not heard her. It seemed almost as though it had – for it slackened swiftly, slackened and stopped, not twenty yards from the place where Bobbie's two flags waved over the line. She saw the great black engine stop dead, but somehow she could not stop waving the flags. And when the driver and the fireman had got off the engine and Peter and Phyllis had gone to meet them and pour out their excited tale of the awful mound just round the corner, Bobbie still waved the flags but more and more feebly and jerkily.

When the others turned towards her she was lying across the line with her hands flung forward and still gripping the sticks of the little red flannel flags.

The engine driver picked her up, carried her to the train, and laid her on the cushions of a first-class carriage.

'Gone right off in a faint,' he said, 'poor little woman. And no wonder. I'll just 'ave a look at this 'ere mound of yours, and then we'll run you back to the station and get her seen to.'

It was horrible to see Bobbie lying so white and quiet, with her lips blue, and parted.

'I believe that's what people look like when they're dead,' whispered Phyllis.

'DON'T!' said Peter, sharply.

They sat by Bobbie on the blue cushions, and the train

ran back. Before it reached their station Bobbie had sighed and opened her eyes, and rolled herself over and begun to cry. This cheered the others wonderfully. They had seen her cry before, but they had never seen her faint, nor anyone else, for the matter of that. They had not known what to do when she was fainting, but now she was only crying they could thump her on the back and tell her not to, just as they always did. And presently, when she stopped crying, they were able to laugh at her for being such a coward as to faint.

When the station was reached, the three were the heroes of an agitated meeting on the platform.

The praises they got for their 'prompt action', their 'common sense', their 'ingenuity', were enough to have turned anybody's head. Phyllis enjoyed herself thoroughly. She had never been a real heroine before, and the feeling was delicious. Peter's ears got very red. Yet he, too, enjoyed himself. Only Bobbie wished they all wouldn't. She wanted to get away.

'You'll hear from the company about this, I expect,' said the station master.

Bobbie wished she might never hear of it again. She pulled at Peter's jacket.

'Oh, come away, come away! I want to go home,' she said.

So they went. And as they went station master and

porter and guards and driver and fireman and passengers sent up a cheer.

'Oh, listen,' cried Phyllis; 'that's for US!'

'Yes,' said Peter. 'I say, I am glad I thought about something red, and waving it.'

'How lucky we DID put on our red flannel petticoats!' said Phyllis.

Bobbie said nothing. She was thinking of the horrible mound, and the trustful train rushing towards it.

'And it was US that saved them,' said Peter.

'How dreadful if they had all been killed!' said Phyllis; 'wouldn't it, Bobbie?'

'We never got any cherries, after all,' said Bobbie.

The others thought her rather heartless.

JANE EYRE

Charlotte Brontë

Orphan Jane Eyre lives with the Reeds, her uncle's family, even though they do not want her and treat her cruelly. One day, as punishment after she hits her cousin John in self-defence, she is locked in the red bedroom in which her uncle died. Jane thinks she sees her uncle's ghost and faints in terror. After this, she is sent away to a boarding school for orphan girls called Lowood. The school is harsh – the girls are given burnt porridge for breakfast, and have to wash in water that has frozen overnight – but Jane is glad to make friends with a kind girl called Helen Burns. One day a benefactor of Lowood, Mr Brocklehurst, arrives to inspect the school and its pupils. Jane knows that Mr and Mrs Reed have told lies to Mr Brocklehurst about what a wicked girl she is, and that Mr Brocklehurst promised to share the information with the teachers. The extract below begins in the classroom as Jane tries to avoid catching Mr Brocklehurst's attention.

I had sat well back on the form, and while seeming to be busy with my sum, had held my slate in such a manner as to conceal my face: I might have escaped notice, had not my treacherous slate somehow happened to slip from my hand, and falling with an obtrusive crash, directly drawn every eye upon me; I knew it was all over now, and, as I stooped to pick up the two fragments of slate, I rallied my forces for the worst. It came.

'A careless girl!' said Mr Brocklehurst, and immediately after – 'It is the new pupil, I perceive.' And before I could draw breath, 'I must not forget I have a word to say respecting her.' Then aloud: how loud it seemed to me! 'Let the child who broke her slate come forward!'

Of my own accord I could not have stirred; I was paralysed: but the two great girls who sit on each side of me, set me on my legs and pushed me towards the dread judge, and then Miss Temple gently assisted me to his very feet, and I caught her whispered counsel.

'Don't be afraid, Jane, I saw it was an accident; you shall not be punished.'

The kind whisper went to my heart like a dagger.

Another minute, and she will despise me for a hypocrite, thought I; and an impulse of fury against Reed, Brocklehurst, and co. bounded in my pulses at the conviction. I was no Helen Burns.

'Fetch that stool,' said Mr Brocklehurst, pointing to a very high one from which a monitor had just risen: it was brought.

'Place the child upon it.'

And I was placed there, by whom I don't know: I was in no condition to note particulars; I was only aware that they had hoisted me up to the height of Mr Brocklehurst's nose, that he was within a yard of me, and that a spread of shot orange and purple silk pelisses and a cloud of silvery plumage extended and waved below me.

Mr Brocklehurst hemmed.

'Ladies,' said he, turning to his family, 'Miss Temple, teachers, and children, you all see this girl?'

Of course they did; for I felt their eyes directed like burning-glasses against my scorched skin.

'You see she is yet young; you observe she possesses the ordinary form of childhood; God has graciously given her the shape that He has given to all of us; no single deformity points her out as a marked character. Who would think that the Evil One had already found a servant and agent in her? Yet such, I grieve to say, is the case.'

A pause – in which I began to steady the palsy of my nerves, and to feel that the Rubicon was passed; and that the trial, no longer to be shirked, must be firmly sustained.

'My dear children,' pursued the black marble clergyman, with pathos, 'this is a sad, a melancholy occasion; for it becomes my duty to warn you, that this girl, who might be one of God's own lambs, is a little castaway: not a member of the true flock, but evidently an interloper and an alien. You must be on your guard against her; you must shun her example; if necessary, avoid her company, exclude her from your sports, and shut her out from your converse. Teachers, you must watch her: keep your eyes on her movements, weigh well her words, scrutinise her actions, punish her body to save her soul: if, indeed, such salvation be possible, for (my tongue falters while I tell it) this girl, this child, the native of a Christian land, worse than many a little heathen who says its prayers to Brahma and kneels before Juggernaut – this girl is – a liar!'

Now came a pause of ten minutes, during which I, by this time in perfect possession of my wits, observed all the female Brocklehursts produce their pocket-handkerchiefs and apply them to their optics, while the elderly lady swayed herself to and fro, and the two younger ones whispered, 'How shocking!'

Mr Brocklehurst resumed. 'This I learnt from her benefactress; from the pious and charitable lady who adopted her in her orphan state, reared her as her own daughter, and whose kindness, whose generosity the unhappy girl repaid by an ingratitude so bad, so dreadful, that at last her excellent patroness was obliged to separate her from her own young ones, fearful lest her vicious example should contaminate their purity: she has sent her here to be healed, even as the Jews of old sent their diseased to the troubled pool of Bethesda; and, teachers, superintendent, I beg of you not to allow the waters to stagnate round her.'

With this sublime conclusion, Mr Brocklehurst adjusted the top button of his surtout, muttered something to his family, who rose, bowed to Miss Temple, and then all the great people sailed in state from the room.

Turning at the door, my judge said, 'Let her stand half an hour longer on that stool, and let no one speak to her during the remainder of the day.'

There was I, then, mounted aloft; I, who had said I could not bear the shame of standing on my natural feet in the middle of the room, was now exposed to general view on a pedestal of infamy. What my sensations were no language can describe; but just as they all rose, stifling my breath and constricting my throat, a girl came up and passed me: in passing, she lifted her eyes. What a strange light inspired them! What an extraordinary sensation that ray sent through me! How the new feeling bore me up! It was as if a martyr, a hero, had passed a slave or victim, and imparted strength in the transit. I mastered the rising hysteria, lifted up my head, and took a firm stand on the stool. Helen Burns asked some slight question about her work of Miss Smith, was chidden for the triviality of the inquiry, returned to her place, and smiled at me as she again went by. What a smile! I remember it now, and I know that it was the effluence of fine intellect, of true courage; it lit up her marked lineaments, her thin face, her sunken grey eye, like a reflection from the aspect of an angel. Yet at that moment Helen Burns wore on her arm 'the untidy badge'; scarcely an hour ago I had heard her condemned by Miss Scatcherd to a dinner of bread and water on the morrow because she had blotted an exercise in copying it out. Such is the imperfect nature of man! Such spots are there on the disc of the clearest planet; and eyes like Miss Scatcherd's can only see those minute defects, and are blind to the full brightness of the orb.

Ere the half-hour ended, five o'clock struck; school was dismissed, and all were gone into the refectory to tea. I now ventured to descend: it was deep dusk; I retired into a corner and sat down on the floor. The spell by which I had been so far supported began to dissolve; reaction took place, and soon, so overwhelming was the grief that seized me, I sank prostrate with my face to the ground.

Now I wept: Helen Burns was not here; nothing sustained me; left to myself I abandoned myself, and my tears watered the boards. I had meant to be so good, and to do so much at Lowood: to make so many friends, to earn respect and win affection. Already I had made visible progress: that very morning I had reached the head of my class; Miss Miller had praised me warmly; Miss Temple had smiled approbation; she had promised to teach me drawing, and to let me learn French, if I continued to make similar improvement two months longer: and then I was well received by my fellow pupils; treated as an equal by those of my own age, and not molested by any; now, here I lay again crushed and trodden on; and could I ever rise more?

Never, I thought; and ardently I wished to die. While sobbing out this wish in broken accents, someone approached: I started up – again Helen Burns was near me; the fading fires just showed her coming up the long, vacant room; she brought my coffee and bread.

'Come, eat something,' she said; but I put both away from me, feeling as if a drop or a crumb would have choked me in my present condition. Helen regarded me, probably with surprise: I could not now abate my agitation, though I tried hard; I continued to weep aloud. She sat down on the ground near me, embraced her knees with her arms, and rested her head upon them;

in that attitude she remained silent. I was the first who spoke.

'Helen, why do you stay with a girl whom everybody believes to be a liar?'

'Everybody, Jane? Why, there are only eighty people who have heard you called so, and the world contains hundreds of millions.'

'But what have I to do with millions? The eighty, I know, despise me.'

'Jane, you are mistaken: probably not one in the school either despises or dislikes you: many, I am sure, pity you much.'

'How can they pity me after what Mr Brocklehurst has said?'

'Mr Brocklehurst is not a god: nor is he even a great and admired man: he is little liked here; he never took steps to make himself liked. Had he treated you as an especial favourite, you would have found enemies, declared or covert, all around you; as it is, the greater number would offer you sympathy if they dared. Teachers and pupils may look coldly on you for a day or two, but friendly feelings are concealed in their hearts; and if you persevere in doing well, these feelings will ere long appear so much the more evidently for their temporary suppression. Besides, Jane' – she paused.

'Well, Helen?' said I, putting my hand into hers: she

chafed my fingers gently to warm them, and went on, 'If all the world hated you, and believed you wicked, while your own conscience approved you, and absolved you from guilt, you would not be without friends.'

'No; I know I should think well of myself; but that is not enough: if others don't love me I would rather die than live – I cannot bear to be solitary and hated, Helen. Look here; to gain some real affection from you, or Miss Temple, or any other whom I truly love, I would willingly submit to have the bone of my arm broken, or to let a bull toss me, or to stand behind a kicking horse, and let it dash its hoof at my chest—'

'Hush, Jane! You think too much of the love of human beings; you are too impulsive, too vehement; the sovereign hand that created your frame, and put life into it, has provided you with other resources than your feeble self, or than creatures feeble as you. Besides this earth, and besides the race of men, there is an invisible world and a kingdom of spirits: that world is round us, for it is everywhere; and those spirits watch us, for they are commissioned to guard us; and if we were dying in pain and shame, if scorn smote us on all sides, and hatred crushed us, angels see our tortures, recognise our innocence (if innocent we be: as I know you are of this charge which Mr Brocklehurst has weakly and pompously repeated at second-hand from Mrs Reed;

for I read a sincere nature in your ardent eyes and on your clear front), and God waits only the separation of spirit from flesh to crown us with a full reward. Why, then, should we ever sink overwhelmed with distress, when life is so soon over, and death is so certain an entrance to happiness – to glory?'

I was silent; Helen had calmed me; but in the tranquillity she imparted there was an alloy of inexpressible sadness. I felt the impression of woe as she spoke, but I could not tell whence it came; and when, having done speaking, she breathed a little fast and coughed a short cough, I momentarily forgot my own sorrows to yield to a vague concern for her.

Resting my head on Helen's shoulder, I put my arms round her waist; she drew me to her, and we reposed in silence. We had not sat long thus, when another person came in. Some heavy clouds, swept from the sky by a rising wind, had left the moon bare; and her light, streaming in through a window near, shone full both on us and on the approaching figure, which we at once recognised as Miss Temple.

'I came on purpose to find you, Jane Eyre,' said she; 'I want you in my room; and as Helen Burns is with you, she may come too.'

We went; following the superintendent's guidance, we had to thread some intricate passages, and mount a staircase before we reached her apartment; it contained a good fire, and looked cheerful. Miss Temple told Helen Burns to be seated in a low armchair on one side of the hearth, and herself taking another, she called me to her side.

'Is it all over?' she asked, looking down at my face. 'Have you cried your grief away?'

'I am afraid I never shall do that.'

'Why?'

'Because I have been wrongly accused; and you, ma'am, and everybody else, will now think me wicked.'

'We shall think you what you prove yourself to be, my child. Continue to act as a good girl, and you will satisfy us.'

'Shall I, Miss Temple?'

'You will,' said she, passing her arm round me. 'And now tell me who is the lady whom Mr Brocklehurst called your benefactress?'

'Mrs Reed, my uncle's wife. My uncle is dead, and he left me to her care.'

'Did she not, then, adopt you of her own accord?'

'No, ma'am; she was sorry to have to do it: but my uncle, as I have often heard the servants say, got her to promise before he died that she would always keep me.'

'Well now, Jane, you know, or at least I will tell you, that when a criminal is accused, he is always allowed to speak in his own defence. You have been charged with falsehood; defend yourself to me as well as you can. Say whatever your memory suggests is true; but add nothing and exaggerate nothing.'

I resolved, in the depth of my heart, that I would be most moderate – most correct; and, having reflected a few minutes in order to arrange coherently what I had to say, I told her all the story of my sad childhood. Exhausted by emotion, my language was more subdued than it generally was when it developed that sad theme; and mindful of Helen's warnings against the indulgence of resentment, I infused into the narrative far less of gall and wormwood than ordinary. Thus restrained and simplified, it sounded more credible: I felt as I went on that Miss Temple fully believed me.

In the course of the tale I had mentioned Mr Lloyd as having come to see me after the fit: for I never forgot the, to me, frightful episode of the red room: in detailing which, my excitement was sure, in some degree, to break bounds; for nothing could soften in my recollection the spasm of agony which clutched my heart when Mrs Reed spurned my wild supplication for pardon, and locked me a second time in the dark and haunted chamber.

I had finished: Miss Temple regarded me a few minutes in silence; she then said –

'I know something of Mr Lloyd; I shall write to him; if his reply agrees with your statement, you shall be publicly cleared from every imputation; to me, Jane, you are clear now.'

KATE CRACKERNUTS

Joseph Jacobs

Joseph Jacobs is listed as the author here, but although he wrote this version of the story in his collection English Fairy Tales, *this Scottish tale already existed, told from person to person, and the true author is unknown. The story includes some words you may not recognise: 'minnie' means 'mother', 'cappy' means 'wooden cup' and a 'henwife' is a woman who raises chickens and other poultry.*

Once upon a time there was a king and a queen, as in many lands have been. The king had a daughter, Anne, and the queen had one named Kate, but Anne was far bonnier than the queen's daughter, though they loved one another like real sisters. The queen was jealous of the king's daughter being bonnier than her own and cast about to spoil her beauty. So she took counsel of the henwife, who told her to send the lassie to her next morning fasting.

So next morning early, the queen said to Anne, 'Go, my dear, to the henwife in the glen, and ask her for some eggs.' So Anne set out, but as she passed through the kitchen she saw a crust, and she took and munched it as she went along.

When she came to the henwife's she asked for eggs, as she had been told to do; the henwife said to her, 'Lift the lid off that pot there and see.' The lassie did so, but nothing happened. 'Go home to your minnie and tell her to keep her larder door better locked,' said the henwife. So she went home to the queen and told her what the henwife had said. The queen knew from this that the lassie had had something to eat, so watched the next morning and sent her away fasting; but the princess saw some country folk picking peas by the roadside and being very kind, she spoke to them and took a handful of the peas, which she ate by the way.

When she came to the henwife's, she said, 'Lift the lid off the pot and you'll see.' So Anne lifted the lid but nothing happened. Then the henwife was rare angry and said to Anne, 'Tell your minnie the pot won't boil if the fire's away.' So Anne went home and told the queen.

The third day the queen goes along with the girl herself to the henwife. Now, this time, when Anne lifted the lid off the pot, off falls her own pretty head, and on jumps a sheep's head.

So the queen was now quite satisfied, and went back home.

Her own daughter, Kate, however, took a fine linen cloth and wrapped it round her sister's head and took her by the hand and they both went out to seek their fortune. They went on, and they went on, and they went on, till they came to a castle. Kate knocked at the door and asked for a night's lodging for herself and a sick sister. They went in and found it was a king's castle, who had two sons, and one of them was sickening away to death and no one could find out what ailed him. And the curious thing was that whoever watched him at night was never seen any more. So the king had offered a peck of silver to anyone who would stop up with him. Now Kate was a very brave girl, so she offered to sit up with him.

Till midnight all went well. As twelve o'clock rang, however, the sick prince rose, dressed himself, and slipped downstairs. Kate followed, but he didn't seem to notice her. The prince went to the stable, saddled his horse, called his hound, jumped into the saddle, and Kate leapt lightly up behind him. Away rode the prince and Kate through the greenwood, Kate, as they pass, plucking nuts from the trees and filling her apron with them. They rode on and on till they came to a green hill. The prince here drew bridle and spoke, 'Open, open, green hill, and let the young prince in with his horse and his hound,' and Kate added, 'And his lady him behind.'

Immediately the green hill opened and they passed in. The prince entered a magnificent hall, brightly lit up, and many beautiful fairies surrounded the prince and led him off to the dance. Meanwhile, Kate, without being noticed, hid herself behind the door. There she saw the prince dancing, and dancing, and dancing, till he could dance no longer and fell upon a couch. Then the fairies would fan him till he could rise again and go on dancing.

At last the cock crew, and the prince made all haste to get on horseback; Kate jumped up behind, and home they rode. When the morning sun rose, the king's servants came in and found Kate sitting down by the fire and cracking her nuts. Kate said the prince had a good night, but she would not sit up another night unless she was to get a peck of gold.

The second night passed as the first had done. The prince got up at midnight and rode away to the green hill and the fairy ball, and Kate went with him, gathering nuts as they rode through the forest. This time she did not watch the prince, for she knew he would dance and dance and dance. But she saw a fairy baby playing with a wand, and overheard one of the fairies say, 'Three strokes of that wand would make Kate's sick sister as bonnie as ever she was.' So Kate rolled nuts to the fairy baby, and rolled nuts till the baby toddled after the nuts and let fall the wand, and Kate took it up and put it in her apron. And at cockcrow they rode home as before, and the moment Kate got home to her room she rushed and touched Anne three times with the wand, and the nasty sheep's head fell off and she was her own pretty self again.

The third night Kate consented to watch, only if she should marry the sick prince. All went on as on the first two nights. This time the fairy baby was playing with a birdie; Kate heard one of the fairies say, 'Three bites of that birdie would make the sick prince as well as ever he was.' Kate rolled all the nuts she had to the fairy baby till the birdie was dropped, and Kate put it in her apron.

At cockcrow they set off again, but instead of cracking her nuts as she used to do, this time Kate plucked the feathers off and cooked the birdie. Soon there arose a very savoury smell.

'Oh!' said the sick prince, 'I wish I had a bite of that birdie,' so Kate gave him a bite of the birdie, and he rose up on his elbow. By and by he cried out again, 'Oh, if I had another bite of that birdie!' So Kate gave him another bite, and he sat up on his bed. Then he said again, 'Oh! if I only had a third bite of that birdie!' So Kate gave him a third bite, and he rose quite well, dressed himself, and sat down by the fire, and when the folk came in next morning they found Kate and the young prince cracking nuts together.

Meanwhile his brother had seen Annie and had fallen in love with her, as everybody did who saw her sweet pretty face. So the sick son married the well sister, and the well son married the sick sister, and they all lived happy and died happy, and never drank out of a dry cappy.

REBECCA of SUNNYBROOK FARM

Kate Douglas Wiggin

Rebecca Rowena Randall is the second oldest of seven children in the Sunnybrook Farm family. Their father is dead and the family is poor, so Rebecca is sent to live with her aunts Miranda and Jane in a village called Hillboro. Miranda and Jane don't want Rebecca to live with them – they prefer her older sister, Hannah, who is practical and good at housework, unlike Rebecca. The story follows Rebecca's ups and downs as she learns these skills and earns the love and respect of her aunts, as well as her trials and triumphs at school as she makes friends and encounters bullies – which we'll see in the extract below. It begins by introducing the Simpson family. The father, Mr Abner Simpson, is currently in prison for stealing a sleigh belonging to his neighbour, Widow Rideout.

Mrs Simpson, who was decidedly Abner's better half, took in washing and went out to do days' cleaning, and the town helped in the feeding and clothing of the children. George, a lanky boy of fourteen, did chores on neighbouring farms, and the others, Samuel, Clara Belle, Susan, Elijah and Elisha, went to school, when sufficiently clothed and not otherwise more pleasantly engaged.

There were no secrets in the villages that lay along the banks of Pleasant River. There were many hard-working people among the inhabitants, but life wore away so quietly and slowly that there was a good deal of spare time for conversation – under the trees at noon in the hayfield; hanging over the bridge at nightfall; seated about the stove in the village store of an evening. These meeting places furnished ample ground for the discussion of current events as viewed by the masculine eye, while choir rehearsals, sewing societies, reading circles, church picnics and the like, gave opportunity for the expression of feminine opinion. All this was taken very much for granted, as a rule, but now and then some supersensitive person made violent objections to it, as a theory of life.

Delia Weeks, for example, was a maiden lady who did dressmaking in a small way; she fell ill, and although attended by all the physicians in the neighbourhood, was sinking slowly into a decline when her cousin Cyrus asked her to come and keep house for him in Lewiston. She went, and in a year grew into a robust, hearty, cheerful woman. Returning to Riverboro on a brief visit, she was asked if she meant to end her days away from home.

'I do most certainly, if I can get any other place to stay,' she responded candidly. 'I was bein' worn to a shadder here, tryin' to keep my little secrets to myself, an' never succeedin'. First they had it I wanted to marry the minister, and when he took a wife in Standish I was known to be disappointed. Then for five or six years they suspicioned I was tryin' for a place to teach school, and when I gave up hope, an' took to dressmakin', they pitied me and sympathised with me for that. When father died I was bound I'd never let anybody know how I was left, for that spites 'em worse than anything else; but there's ways o' findin' out, an' they found out, hard as I fought 'em! Then there was my brother James that went to Arizona when he was sixteen. I gave good news of him for thirty years runnin', but aunt Achsy Tarbox had a ferretin' cousin that went out to Tombstone for her health, and she wrote to a postmaster, or to some kind of a town authority, and found Jim and wrote back aunt Achsy all about him and just how unfortunate he'd been. They knew when I had my teeth out and a new set made; they knew when I put on a false front-piece; they knew when the fruit peddler asked me to be his third wife – I never told 'em, an' you can be sure *he* never did, but they don't *need* to be told in this village; they have nothin' to do but guess, an' they'll guess right every time. I was all tuckered out tryin' to mislead 'em and deceive 'em and sidetrack 'em; but the minute I got where I wa'n't put under a microscope by day an' a telescope by night and had myself *to* myself without sayin' 'By your leave,' I begun to pick up. Cousin Cyrus is an old man an' consid'able trouble, but he thinks my teeth are handsome an' says I've got a splendid suit of hair. There ain't a person in Lewiston that knows about the minister, or father's will, or Jim's doin's, or the fruit peddler; an' if they should find out, they wouldn't care, an' they couldn't remember; for Lewiston's a busy place, thanks be!'

Miss Delia Weeks may have exaggerated matters somewhat, but it is easy to imagine that Rebecca as well as all the other Riverboro children had heard the particulars of the Widow Rideout's missing sleigh and Abner Simpson's supposed connection with it.

There is not an excess of delicacy or chivalry in the ordinary country school, and several choice conundrums and bits of verse dealing with the Simpson affair were bandied about among the scholars, uttered always, be it said to their credit, in undertones, and when the Simpson children were not in the group.

Rebecca Randall was of precisely the same stock, and

had had much the same associations as her schoolmates, so one can hardly say why she so hated mean gossip and so instinctively held herself aloof from it.

Among the Riverboro girls of her own age was a certain excellently named Minnie Smellie, who was anything but a general favourite. She was a ferret-eyed, blonde-haired, spindle-legged little creature whose mind was a cross between that of a parrot and a sheep. She was suspected of copying answers from other girls' slates, although she had never been caught in the act. Rebecca and Emma Jane always knew when she had brought a tart or a triangle of layer cake with her school luncheon, because on those days she forsook the cheerful society of her mates and sought a safe solitude in the woods, returning after a time with a jocund smile on her smug face.

After one of these private luncheons Rebecca had been tempted beyond her strength, and when Minnie took her seat among them asked, 'Is your headache better, Minnie? Let me wipe off that strawberry jam over your mouth.'

There was no jam there as a matter of fact, but the guilty Minnie's handkerchief went to her crimson face in a flash.

Rebecca confessed to Emma Jane that same afternoon that she felt ashamed of her prank. 'I do hate her ways,' she exclaimed, 'but I'm sorry I let her know we 'spected her; and so to make up, I gave her that little piece of broken coral I keep in my bead purse; you know the one?'

'It don't hardly seem as if she deserved that, and her so greedy,' remarked Emma Jane.

'I know it, but it makes me feel better,' said Rebecca largely; 'and then I've had it two years, and it's broken so it wouldn't ever be any real good, beautiful as it is to look at.'

The coral had partly served its purpose as a reconciling bond, when one afternoon Rebecca, who had stayed after school for her grammar lesson as usual, was returning home by way of the short cut. Far ahead, beyond the bars, she espied the Simpson children just entering the woodsy bit. Seesaw was not with them, so she hastened her steps in order to secure company on her homeward walk. They were speedily lost to view, but when she had almost overtaken them she heard, in the trees beyond, Minnie Smellie's voice lifted high in song, and the sound of a child's sobbing. Clara Belle, Susan and the twins were running along the path, and Minnie was dancing up and down, shrieking:

'"*What made the sleigh love Simpson so?*"
The eager children cried.
"*Why, Simpson loved the sleigh, you know,*"

The teacher quick replied.'

The last glimpse of the routed Simpson tribe, and the last flutter of their tattered garments, disappeared in the dim distance. The fall of one small stone cast by the valiant Elijah, known as 'the fighting twin', did break the stillness of the woods for a moment, but it did not come within a hundred yards of Minnie, who shouted 'Jail birds!' at the top of her lungs and then turned, with an agreeable feeling of excitement, to meet Rebecca, standing perfectly still in the path, with a day of reckoning plainly set forth in her blazing eyes.

Minnie's face was not pleasant to see, for a coward detected at the moment of wrongdoing is not an object of delight.

'Minnie Smellie, if ever – I – catch – you – singing – that – to the Simpsons again – do you know what I'll do?' asked Rebecca in a tone of concentrated rage.

'I don't know and I don't care,' said Minnie jauntily, though her looks belied her.

'I'll take that piece of coral away from you, and I THINK I shall slap you besides!'

'You wouldn't darst,' retorted Minnie. 'If you do, I'll tell my mother and the teacher, so there!'

'I don't care if you tell your mother, my mother, and all your relations, and the president,' said Rebecca, gaining courage as the noble words fell from her lips. 'I don't care if you tell the town, the whole of York county, the state of Maine and – and the nation!' she finished grandiloquently. 'Now you run home and remember what I say. If you do it again, and especially if you say "jail birds", if I think it's right and my duty, I shall punish you somehow.'

The next morning at recess Rebecca observed Minnie telling the tale with variations to Huldah Meserve. 'She *threatened* me,' whispered Minnie, 'but I never believe a word she says.'

The latter remark was spoken with the direct intention of being overheard, for Minnie had spasms of bravery, when well surrounded by the machinery of law and order.

As Rebecca went back to her seat she asked Miss Dearborn if she might pass a note to Minnie Smellie and received permission. This was the note:

Of all the girls that are so mean
There's none like Minnie Smellie.
I'll take away the gift I gave
And pound her into jelly.

P. S. Now do you believe me?
R. Randall.

The effect of this piece of doggerel was entirely convincing, and for days afterwards whenever Minnie met the Simpsons even a mile from the brick house she shuddered and held her peace.

FIVE on a
TREASURE ISLAND

Enid Blyton

The Famous Five are Julian, Dick, George, Anne and Timmy the dog. George's real name is Georgina, but she insists on the shortened version. She likes to wear boys' clothes, has her hair cut very short, and doesn't mind when people think she is a boy. In fact, she rather enjoys it!

Five on a Treasure Island is the very first adventure the Five have together. They have rowed out to visit Kirrin Island when a storm washes up an old shipwreck. When they explore the shipwreck they find a treasure map showing the location of long-lost gold ingots hidden on the island. But some bad men who are also looking for the gold capture George, Julian and Timmy, and lock them in the dungeons of the island's old castle. Dick and Anne rescue them, and they plan to escape the island...

'Now come on!' said George after a minute. 'Off to the boat. Quick! Those men may be back at any time.'

They rushed to the cove. There was their boat, lying where they had pulled it, out of reach of the waves. But what a shock for them!

'They've taken the oars!' said George in dismay. 'The beasts! They know we can't row the boat away without oars. They were afraid you and Anne might row off, Dick – so instead of bothering to tow the boat behind them, they just grabbed the oars. Now we're stuck. We can't possibly get away.'

It was a great disappointment. The children were almost ready to cry. After Dick's marvellous rescue of George and Julian, it had seemed as if everything was going right – and now suddenly things were going wrong again.

'We must think this out,' said Julian, sitting down where he could see at once if any boat came in sight.

'The men have gone off – probably to get a ship from somewhere in which they can put the ingots and sail away. They won't be back for some time, I should think, because you can't charter a ship all in a hurry – unless, of course, they've got one of their own.'

'And in the meantime we can't get off the island to get help, because they've got our oars,' said George. 'We can't even signal to any passing fishing boat because they won't be out just now. The tide's wrong. It seems as if all we've got to do is wait here patiently till the men come back and take my gold! And we can't stop them.'

'You know – I've got a sort of plan coming into my head,' said Julian slowly. 'Wait a bit – don't interrupt me. I'm thinking.'

The others waited in silence while Julian sat and frowned, thinking of his plan. Then he looked at the others with a smile.

'I believe it will work,' he said. 'Listen! We'll wait here in patience till the men come back. What will they do? They'll drag away those stones at the top of the dungeon entrance, and go down the steps. They'll go to the storeroom, where they left us – thinking we are still there – and they will go into the room. Well, what about one of us being hidden down there ready to bolt them into the room? Then we can either go off in their motorboat or our own boat if they bring back our oars – and get help.'

Anne thought it was a marvellous idea. But Dick and George did not look so certain. 'We'd have to go down and bolt that door again to make it seem as if we are still prisoners there,' said George. 'And suppose the one who hides down there doesn't manage to bolt the men in? It might be very difficult to do that quickly enough. They will simply catch whoever we plan to leave down there – and come up to look for the rest of us.'

'That's true,' said Julian thoughtfully. 'Well, we'll

suppose that Dick, or whoever goes down, doesn't manage to bolt them in and make them prisoners – and the men come up here again. All right – while they are down below we'll pile big stones over the entrance, just as they did. Then they won't be able to get out.'

'What about Dick down below?' said Anne, at once.

'I could climb up the well again!' said Dick eagerly. 'I'll be the one to go down and hide. I'll do my best to bolt the men into the room. And if I have to escape, I'll climb up the well shaft again. The men don't know about that. So even if they are not prisoners in the dungeon room, they'll be prisoners underground!'

The children talked over this plan, and decided that it was the best they could think of. Then George said she thought it would be a good thing to have a meal. They were all half starved and, now that the worry and excitement of being rescued was over, they were feeling very hungry!

They fetched some food from the little room and ate it in the cove, keeping a sharp lookout for the return of the men. After about two hours they saw a big fishing-smack appear in the distance, and heard the chug-chug-chug of a motorboat too.

'There they are!' said Julian in excitement, and he jumped to his feet. 'That's the ship they mean to load with the ingots, and sail away in safety – and there's the motorboat bringing the men back! Quick, Dick, down the well you go, and hide until you hear them in the dungeons!'

Dick shot off. Julian turned to the others. 'We'll have to hide,' he said. 'Now that the tide is out we'll hide over there, behind those uncovered rocks. I don't somehow think the men will do any hunting for Dick and Anne – but they might. Come on! Quick!'

They all hid themselves behind the rocks, and heard the motorboat come chugging into the tiny harbour. They could hear men calling to one another. There sounded to be more than two men this time. Then the men left the inlet and went up the low cliff towards the ruined castle.

Julian crept behind the rocks and peeped to see what the men were doing. He felt certain they were pulling away the slabs of stone that had been piled on top of the entrance to prevent Dick and Anne going down to rescue the others.

'George! Come on!' called Julian in a low tone. 'I think the men have gone down the steps into the dungeons now. We must go and try to put those big stones back. Quick!'

George, Julian and Anne ran softly and swiftly to the old courtyard of the castle. They saw that the stones had been pulled away from the entrance to the dungeons.

The men had disappeared. They had plainly gone down the steps.

The three children did their best to tug at the heavy stones to drag them back. But their strength was not the same as that of the men, and they could not manage to get any very big stones across. They put three smaller ones, and Julian hoped the men would find them too difficult to move from below. 'If only Dick has managed to bolt them into that room!' he said to the others. 'Come on, back to the well now. Dick will have to come up there, because he won't be able to get out of the entrance.'

They all went to the well. Dick had removed the old wooden cover, and it was lying on the ground. The children leant over the hole of the well and waited anxiously. What was Dick doing? They could hear nothing from the well and they longed to know what was happening.

There was plenty happening down below! The two men, and another, had gone down into the dungeons, expecting, of course, to find Julian, George and the dog still locked up in the storeroom with the ingots. They passed the well shaft, not guessing that an excited small boy was hidden there, ready to slip out of the opening as soon as they had passed.

Dick heard them pass. He slipped out of the well opening and followed behind quietly, his feet making no sound. He could see the beams made by the men's powerful torches, and with his heart thumping loudly he crept along the smelly old passage, between great caves, until the men turned into the wide passage where the store-cave lay.

'Here it is,' Dick heard one of the men say, as he flashed his torch on to the great door. 'The gold's in there – so are the kids!'

The men unbolted the door at top and bottom. Dick was glad that he had slipped along to bolt the door, for if he hadn't done that before the men had come they would have known that Julian and George had escaped, and would have been on their guard.

The man opened the door and stepped inside. The second man followed him. Dick crept as close as he dared, waiting for the third man to go in too. Then he meant to slam the door and bolt it!

The first man swung his torch round and gave a loud exclamation. 'The children are gone! How strange! Where are they?'

Two of the men were now in the cave – and the third stepped in at that moment. Dick darted forward and slammed the door. It made a crash that went echoing round and round the caves and passages. Dick fumbled with the bolts, his hand trembling. They were stiff and rusty. The boy found it hard to shoot them home in their sockets. And meanwhile the men were not idle!

As soon as they heard the door slam they spun round. The third man put his shoulder to the door at once and heaved hard. Dick had just got one of the bolts almost into its socket. Then all three men forced their strength against the door, and the bolt gave way!

Dick stared in horror. The door was opening! He turned and fled down the dark passage. The men flashed their torches on and saw him. They went after the boy at top speed.

Dick fled to the well shaft. Fortunately the opening was on the opposite side, and he could clamber into it without being seen in the light of the torches. The boy only just had time to squeeze through into the shaft before the three men came running by. Not one of them guessed that the runaway was squeezed into the well-shaft they passed! Indeed, the men did not even know that there was a well there.

Trembling from head to foot, Dick began to climb the rope he had left dangling from the rungs of the iron ladder. He undid it when he reached the ladder itself, for he thought that perhaps the men might discover the old well and try to climb up later. They would not be able to do that if there was no rope dangling down.

The boy climbed up the ladder quickly, and squeezed

round the stone slab near the top. The other children were there, waiting for him.

They knew at once by the look on Dick's face that he had failed in what he had tried to do. They pulled him out quickly. 'It was no good,' said Dick, panting with his climb. 'I couldn't do it. They burst the door open just as I was bolting it, and chased me. I got into the shaft just in time.'

'They're trying to get out of the entrance now!' cried Anne suddenly. 'Quick! What shall we do? They'll catch us all!'

'To the boat!' shouted Julian, and he took Anne's hand to help her along. 'Come along! It's our only chance. The men will perhaps be able to move those stones.'

The four children fled down the courtyard. George darted into the little stone room as they passed it, and caught up an axe. Dick wondered why she bothered to do that. Tim dashed along with them, barking madly.

They came to the cove. Their own boat lay there without oars. The motorboat was there too. George jumped into it and gave a yell of delight.

'Here are our oars!' she shouted. 'Take them, Julian, I've got a job to do here! Get the boat down to the water, quick!'

Julian and Dick took the oars. Then they dragged their boat down to the water, wondering what George was doing. All kinds of crashing sounds came from the motorboat!

'George! George! Buck up. The men are out!' suddenly yelled Julian. He had seen the three men running to the cliff that led down to the cove. George leapt out of the motorboat and joined the others. They pushed their boat out on to the water, and George took the oars at once, pulling for all she was worth.

The three men ran to their motorboat. Then they paused in the greatest dismay – for George had completely ruined it! She had chopped wildly with her axe at all the machinery she could see – and now the boat could not possibly be started! It was damaged beyond any repair the men could make with the few tools they had.

'You wicked girl!' yelled Jake, shaking his fist at George. 'Wait till I get you!'

'I'll wait!' shouted back George, her blue eyes shining dangerously. 'And you can wait too! You won't be able to leave my island now!'

The three men stood at the edge of the sea, watching George pull away strongly from the shore. They could do nothing. Their boat was quite useless.

'The fishing smack they've got waiting out there is too big to use in that little inlet,' said George, as she pulled hard at her oars. 'They'll have to stay there till someone goes in with a boat. I guess they're as wild as can be!'

Their boat had to pass fairly near to the big fishing-boat. A man hailed them as they came by.

'Ahoy there! Have you come from Kirrin Island?'

'Don't answer,' said George. 'Don't say a word.' So no one said anything at all, but looked the other way as if they hadn't heard.

'Ahoy there!' yelled the man angrily. 'Are you deaf? Have you come from the island?'

Still the children said nothing at all, but looked away while George rowed steadily. The man on the ship gave it up, and looked in a worried manner towards the island. He felt sure the children had come from there – and he knew enough of his comrades' adventures to wonder if everything was right on the island.

'He may put out a boat from the smack and go and see what's happening,' said George. 'Well, he can't do much except take the men off – with a few ingots! I hardly think they'll dare to take any of the gold, though, now that we've escaped to tell our tale!'

WHITE
CHRYSANTHEMUM

Yei Theodora Ozaki

This story appears in a book called Warriors of Old Japan and Other Stories, *but was originally written as a Chinese-language poem by Inoue Tetsujirō, and then rewritten as a Japanese-language poem by Ochiai Naobumi. The heroine Shiragiku's name can also be translated as White Aster (asters and chrysanthemums are both flowers). In the extract below Shiragiku has left home to search for her father, who went out to hunt some days before and has not returned. After an arduous journey she comes to a shrine where a kind monk offers her a place to rest for the night.*

At the hour when the hush of night is deepest, Shiragiku saw her father enter the room and draw near her pillow. The tears stood in his eyes and in a sad voice he said, 'Shiragiku, I have fallen over a precipice, and now I am at the bottom of a chasm many hundred feet deep. Here the brambles and bamboo grass grow so thick that I am unable to find my way out of the jungle. I may not live till the morrow, so I came to see you for the last time in this world.'

As soon as he had finished speaking, White Chrysanthemum stretched out her hands and tried to catch hold of his sleeves to detain him, crying, 'Father! Father!' But with the sound of her own voice she awoke.

She sprang up expecting to see her father, but there was nothing in the room except the night lantern glimmering faintly. While she was wondering whether the vision were a dream or a reality, the dawn began to break and the beating of a drum throbbed through the temple. White Chrysanthemum rose soon after sunrise, ate the simple breakfast of rice and bean soup she found slipped into her room, and quickly left the temple. She did not wait to see the kind priest, though he had asked her to do so, saying that he would do what he could to help her; for she had remembered his diffidence the night before, and thought that very likely he belonged to a sect which forbade its priests to converse with the world, and she felt sorry that she had disturbed him.

Her dream was so vividly real to her that it seemed as if she heard her father calling to her for help; so making all possible speed she set out once more with the faith and simplicity of childhood to find him. Far off in the woods the bark of a fox could be heard, while along the path the cloudy tufts of the *obana* grass rustled as she passed. Shiragiku shivered as the cold morning wind pierced through her body. As she pursued her way along the rough mountain pass wild creatures scuttled away, frightened, from before her into the woods, and overhead the birds sang to each other in the trees.

At last she reached the top of the pass, to find it covered with clouds, and it seemed to White Chrysanthemum as if they must carry her away with them in their onward sweep. She sat down on a stone to recover her breath, for the climb had been steep. In a few minutes the mists began to clear away. She stood up and looked about her, hoping that she might find some trace of her father, but as far as eye could reach nothing but mountains, range after range, could be seen riding one above the other in the blue sky.

Suddenly a noise in the bushes behind her made White Chrysanthemum start, and before she could flee a band of robbers rushed out upon her. They seized and bound her tightly. She cried out for help, but only the echoes answered her. Down the mountain they led her till they reached the valley; for a whole day they hurried her along till they came to a strange-looking house.

This was in such a neglected condition that moss covered the walls, and it was so closely shut up that the sunbeams never entered the rooms.

As they approached the place, a man who seemed to be the chief of the band came out, and as he caught sight of the maiden, said with an evil smile, 'You've brought a good prize this time!'

The robbers now untied Shiragiku's hands and led her into the house and then into a room where dinner was prepared, with rice and fish and wine in great quantities. Then they all sat down, and as they began to eat, it seemed to her that they were a lot of demons. The chief passed some food to her and pressed her to eat. The long walk in the bracing air of the autumn day had made Shiragiku so hungry that in spite of her fear and distress she was glad of the food. At last, when she had finished her meal, he turned to her and said, 'That you have been caught by my men and brought here must be the work of fate. So now you must look upon me as your husband and serve me all your life. I have a good *koto* harp which I keep with great care, and to show your gratitude for this marriage you will have to play before me often and to cheer me with your songs, for I am fond of music. If you refuse to obey me, I will make your life as hard as climbing a mountain of swords or walking through a forest of needles.'

Shiragiku felt that she would rather die than marry this man, but she could not refuse to play the *koto* for him. The *koto* was brought by one of the men at a word of command from the chief and placed before the girl, who began to strike the chords, her tears falling fast the while. She played so well that even those hard-hearted robbers were touched by her music, and one or two of them whispered together that hers was a hard fate and they wished that they could find some means of saving her.

Outside the house in the shadow of a large tree stood a young man, watching all that went on and listening to the music. By the voice of the singer as she sang, he knew that the player was she whom he sought. No sooner did the music stop than he rushed into the house and attacked the robbers with great fury. Anger gave strength to his onslaught, and the bandits were so taken by surprise that they were paralysed with fear and offered no resistance. In a few minutes the chief was killed, while two others lay senseless on the mats, and the rest ran away.

Then the young man, who was dressed in the black vestments of a priest, took the trembling girl by the hand and led her to a window, through which the moonlight streamed. As Shiragiku gazed up in gratitude and wonder at her deliverer, she saw that he was none other than the young priest of the temple, who had been so kind to her the night before.

'Don't be afraid!' he said quietly and soothingly; 'don't

be afraid! I am no stranger, I am your brother Akihide. Now I will tell you my story, so listen to me.

'You cannot remember me, for you were only a little child of three when my bad conduct roused my father's anger and I ran away from home and started for the capital. I embarked on a small vessel and after sailing along for several days I reached Waka-no-ura, passing the island of Awaji on the way. From Waka-no-ura I proceeded on foot. It was the close of spring and the cherry blossoms were falling, and the ground was covered with the pink snow of their petals; but there was nothing of the joy of spring in my heart, which was heavy at the thought of my parents' displeasure and the fearful step I had just taken. As soon as I reached the capital, I put myself under the charge of a priest and went through a severe course of study, for I had already repented of my idle ways and longed to do better. Under my good master's guidance I learnt the way of virtue. My heart was softened by knowledge, and when I remembered the love of my parents, I regretted my evil past and never did the sun go down but I wept in secret over it.

'So the years went by. At last the pain of homesickness became so great that I determined to return home and beg my parents' forgiveness. I hoped and planned to devote myself to them in their old age and to make amends in the future for the shortcomings of the past. But insurmountable difficulties beset me in my new-formed purpose. War had broken out, and the face of the country was entirely changed. Cities were turned into wildernesses, weeds grew tall and thick all over the roads, and when I reached our province it was impossible to find either the old home or anyone who could give me the slightest clue as to the whereabouts of you all. Life became a burden to me. You may imagine something of what I felt, but my tongue fails to describe my misery. I was desolate with no one belonging to me, so I resolved to forsake the world and become a priest, and after wandering about I took up my abode in that old temple where you found me. But even the religious life could not still my remorse. I was haunted by the fear of what had become of my father and mother and sister. Were they alive or were they dead? Should I ever see them again? These were the questions which tormented me ceaselessly.

'Morning and evening, I prayed before the shrine in the room where you slept last night – prayed that I might have news of you all. Great is the mercy of Buddha! Imagine the mingled joy and sorrow I felt when you came yesterday and told me of all that had happened since I left home. I was about to make myself known to you, but I was too ashamed to do so. It was, however, harder for me to conceal my secret than it would have been to tell it, for I longed to do so with my whole heart and soul. In the morning when I came to the room and found you gone, I followed after you in fear lest you should fall into the hands of the bandits who haunt these hills and thus it was that I saved you.

'You can never know how glad I am to have done this for you, but alas! I am ashamed to meet my father because of the remembrance of the past! Had I done my duty as a son, had I never run away wickedly from home, how much suffering I might have saved my mother and you, poor Shiragiku! Terrible indeed is my sin!' And with these words the young man drew out a short sword and was about to take his own life.

When Shiragiku saw what he was going to do, she gave a loud cry and springing to his side seized his hands with all her strength and stopped him from doing the dread deed. With tender sisterly words she tried to comfort him, telling him that she knew his father had forgiven him, and was living in the daily hope of his return – that the happiness and solace he could now give him in his old age would more than atone for the past; she begged him to remember his mother's dying prayer that he would establish their house and keep up the ancestral rites before the family shrine when his parents were dead. As she spoke, he desisted from his desperate purpose. The peace of night and the stillness of the moonlit world around them brought balm to both their troubled hearts, and as they bade each other goodnight the silence was unbroken save for the cry of the wild geese as they flew across the sky.

UNDERSTOOD BETSY

Dorothy Canfield Fisher

Elizabeth Ann is an orphan who moves from Aunt Harriet's home in the city to Aunt Abigail and Uncle Henry's farm in Vermont. They give her the nickname Betsy, and while at first she is pale and timid, the fresh air and outdoor life on the farm start to give her strength. In the extract below Betsy comes home in tears after doing badly in a school exam, but receives no sympathy from Cousin Ann. Ann tells her there's no point being upset, because Hemlock Mountain will still stand even if she does fail an exam. Confused by what she means, Betsy goes outside to enjoy a treat of hot maple syrup poured on fresh snow.

She found a clean white snow bank under a pine tree, and, setting her cup of syrup down in a safe place, began to pat the snow down hard to make the right bed for the waxing of the syrup. The sun, very hot for that late March day, brought out strongly the tarry perfume of the big pine tree. Near her the sap dripped musically into a bucket, already half full, hung on a maple tree. A blue jay rushed suddenly through the upper branches of the wood, his screaming and chattering voice sounding like noisy children at play.

Elizabeth Ann took up her cup and poured some of the thick, hot syrup out on the hard snow, making loops and curves as she poured. It stiffened and hardened at once, and she lifted up a great coil of it, threw her head back and let it drop into her mouth. Concentrated sweetness of summer days was in that mouthful, part of it still hot and aromatic, part of it icy and wet with melting snow. She crunched it all together with her strong child's teeth into a delicious, big lump and sucked on it dreamily, her eyes on the rim of Hemlock Mountain, high above her there, the snow on it bright golden in the sunlight. Uncle Henry had promised to take her up to the top as soon as the snow went off. She wondered what the top of a mountain would be like. Uncle Henry had said the main thing was that you could see so much of the world at once. He said it was too queer the way your own house and big barn and great fields looked like little toy things that weren't of any account. It was because you could see so much more than just the . . .

She heard an imploring whine, and a cold nose was thrust into her hand! Why, there was old Shep begging for his share of waxed sugar. He loved it, though it did stick to his teeth so! She poured out another lot and gave half of it to Shep. It immediately stuck his jaws together tight, and he began pawing at his mouth and shaking his head till Betsy had to laugh. Then he managed to pull his jaws apart and chewed loudly and visibly, tossing his head, opening his mouth wide till Betsy could see the sticky, brown candy draped in melting festoons all over his big white teeth and red gullet. Then with a gulp he had swallowed it all down and was whining for more, striking softly at the little girl's skirt with his forepaw. 'Oh, you eat it too fast!' cried Betsy, but she shared her next lot with him too. The sun had gone down over Hemlock Mountain by this time, and the big slope above her was all deep blue shadow. The mountain looked much higher now as the dusk began to fall and loomed up bigger and bigger as though it reached to the sky. It was no wonder houses looked small from its top. Betsy ate the last of her sugar, looking up at the quiet giant there, towering grandly above her. There was no lump in her throat now. And, although she still thought she did not know what in the world Cousin Ann meant by saying that about Hemlock Mountain and her examination, it's my opinion that she had made a very good beginning of an understanding.

She was just picking up her cup to take it back to the sap house when Shep growled a little and stood with his ears and tail up, looking down the road. Something was coming down that road in the blue, clear twilight, something that was making a very queer noise. It sounded almost like somebody crying. It *was* somebody crying! It was a child crying. It was a little, little girl... Betsy could see her now... stumbling along and crying as though her heart would break. Why, it was little Molly, her own particular charge at school, whose reading lesson she heard every day. Betsy and Shep ran to meet her. 'What's the matter, Molly? What's the matter?' Betsy knelt down and put her arms around the weeping child. 'Did you fall down? Did you hurt you? What are you doing way off here? Did you lose your way?'

'I don't want to go away! I don't want to go away!' said Molly over and over, clinging tightly to Betsy. It was a long time before Betsy could quiet her enough to find out what had happened. Then she made out between Molly's sobs that her mother had been taken suddenly sick and had to go away to a hospital, and that left nobody at home to take care of Molly, and she was to be sent away to some strange relatives in the city who didn't want her at all and who said so right out...

Oh, Elizabeth Ann knew all about that! and her heart swelled big with sympathy. For a moment she stood again out on the sidewalk in front of the Lathrop house with old Mrs Lathrop's ungracious white head bobbing from a window, and knew again that ghastly feeling of being unwanted. Oh, she knew why little Molly was crying! And she shut her hands together hard and made up her mind that she *would* help her out!

'What's the matter, Molly? What's the matter?'

Do you know what she did, right off, without thinking about it? She didn't go and look up Aunt Abigail. She didn't wait till Uncle Henry came back from his round of emptying sap buckets into the big tub on his sled. As fast as her feet could carry her she flew back to Cousin Ann in the sap house. I can't tell you (except again that Cousin Ann was Cousin Ann) why it was that Betsy ran so fast to her and was so sure that everything would be all right as soon as Cousin Ann knew about it; but whatever the reason was it was a good one, for, though Cousin Ann did not stop to kiss Molly or even to look at her more than one sharp first glance, she said after a moment's pause, during which she filled a syrup can and screwed the cover down very tight, 'Well, if her folks will let her stay, how would you like to have Molly come and stay with us till her mother gets back from the hospital? Now you've got a room of your own, I guess if you wanted to you could have her sleep with you.'

'Oh, Molly, Molly, Molly!' shouted Betsy, jumping up and down, and then hugging the little girl with all her might. 'Oh, it will be like having a little sister!'

Cousin Ann sounded a dry, warning note. 'Don't be too sure her folks will let her. We don't know about them yet.'

Betsy ran to her, and caught her hand, looking up at her with shining eyes. 'Cousin Ann, if *you* go to see them and ask them, they will!'

This made even Cousin Ann give a little abashed smile of pleasure, although she made her face grave again at once and said, 'You'd better go along back to the house now, Betsy. It's time for you to help Mother with the supper.'

The two children trotted back along the darkening wood road, Shep running before them, little Molly clinging fast to the older child's hand. 'Aren't you ever afraid, Betsy, in the woods this way?' she asked admiringly, looking about her with timid eyes.

'Oh, no!' said Betsy, protectingly. 'There's nothing to be afraid of, except getting off on the wrong fork of the road, near the Wolf Pit.'

'Oh, *ow!*' said Molly, cringing. 'What's the Wolf Pit? What an awful name!'

Betsy laughed. She tried to make her laugh sound brave like Cousin Ann's, which always seemed so scornful of being afraid. As a matter of fact, she was beginning to fear that they *had* made the wrong turn, and she was not quite sure that she could find the way home. But she put this out of her mind and walked along very fast, peering ahead into the dusk. 'Oh, it hasn't anything to do with wolves,' she said in answer to Molly's question, 'anyhow, not now. It's just a big, deep hole in the ground where a brook had dug out a cave . . . Uncle Henry told me all about it when he showed it to me . . . and then part of the roof caved in; sometimes there's ice in the corner of the covered part all the summer, Aunt Abigail says.'

'Why do you call it the Wolf Pit?' asked Molly, walking very close to Betsy and holding very tightly to her hand.

'Oh, long, ever so long ago, when the first settlers came up here, they heard a wolf howling all night, and when it didn't stop in the morning, they came up here on the mountain and found a wolf had fallen in and couldn't get out.'

'My! I hope they killed him!' said Molly.

'Oh, gracious! That was more than a hundred years ago,' said Betsy. She was not thinking of what she was saying. She was thinking that if they *were* on the right road they ought to be home by this time. She was thinking that the right road ran downhill to the house all the way, and that this certainly seemed to be going up a little. She was wondering what had become of Shep. 'Stand here just a minute, Molly,' she said. 'I want . . . I just want to go ahead a little bit and see . . . and see . . .'

She darted on around a curve of the road and stood still, her heart sinking. The road turned there and led straight up the mountain!

For just a moment the little girl felt a wild impulse to burst out in a shriek for Aunt Frances, and to run crazily away, anywhere so long as she was running. But the thought of Molly standing back there, trustfully waiting to be taken care of, shut Betsy's lips together hard before her scream of fright got out. She stood still, thinking. Now she mustn't get frightened. All they had to do was to walk back along the road till they came to the fork and then make the right turn. But what if they didn't get back to the turn till it was so dark they couldn't see it . . . ? Well, she mustn't think of that. She ran back, calling, 'Come on, Molly,' in a tone she tried to make as firm as Cousin Ann's. 'I guess we have made the wrong turn after all. We'd better . . .'

But there was no Molly there. In the brief moment Betsy had stood thinking, Molly had disappeared. The long, shadowy wood road held not a trace of her.

Then Betsy *was* frightened and then she *did* begin to scream at the top of her voice, 'Molly! Molly!' She was beside herself with terror, and started back hastily to hear Molly's voice, very faint, apparently coming from the ground under her feet.

'Ow! Ow! Betsy! Get me out! Get me out!'

'Where *are* you?' shrieked Betsy.

'I don't know!' came Molly's sobbing voice. 'I just moved the least little bit out of the road, and slipped on the ice and began to slide and I couldn't stop myself and I fell down into a deep hole!'

Betsy's head felt as though her hair were standing up straight on end with horror. Molly must have fallen down into the Wolf Pit! Yes, they were quite near it. She remembered now that big white birch tree stood right at the place where the brook tumbled over the edge and fell into it. Although she was dreadfully afraid of falling in herself, she went cautiously over to this tree, feeling her way with her foot to make sure she did not slip, and peered down into the cavernous gloom below. Yes, there was Molly's little face, just a white speck. The child was crying, sobbing and holding up her arms to Betsy.

'Are you hurt, Molly?'

'No. I fell into a big snow bank, but I'm all wet and frozen and I want to get out! I want to get out!'

Betsy held on to the birch tree. Her head whirled. What *should* she do! 'Look here, Molly,' she called down, 'I'm going to run back along to the right road and back to the house and get Uncle Henry. He'll come with a rope and get you out!'

At this Molly's crying rose to a frantic scream. 'Oh, Betsy, *don't* leave me here alone! Don't! Don't! The wolves will get me! Betsy, don't leave me alone!' The child was wild with terror.

'But *I can't* get you out myself!' screamed back Betsy, crying herself. Her teeth were chattering with the cold.

'Don't go! Don't go!' came up from the darkness of the pit in a piteous howl. Betsy made a great effort and stopped crying. She sat down on a stone and tried to think. And this is what came into her mind as a guide: 'What would Cousin Ann do if she were here? She wouldn't cry. She would *think* of something.'

Betsy looked around her desperately. The first thing she saw was the big limb of a pine tree, broken off by the wind, which half lay and half slantingly stood up against a tree a little distance above the mouth of the pit. It had been there so long that the needles had all dried and fallen off, and the skeleton of the branch with the broken stubs looked like . . . yes, it looked like a ladder! *That* was what Cousin Ann would have done!

'Wait a minute! Wait a minute, Molly!' she called wildly down into the pit, warm all over in excitement. 'Now listen. You go off there in a corner, where the ground makes a sort of roof. I'm going to throw down something you can climb up on, maybe.'

'Ow! Ow, it'll hit me!' cried poor little Molly, more and more frightened. But she scrambled off under her shelter obediently, while Betsy struggled with the branch. It was so firmly embedded in the snow that at first she could not budge it at all. But after she cleared that away and prised hard with the stick she was using as a lever she felt it give a little. She bore down with all her might, throwing her weight again and again on her lever, and finally felt the big branch perceptibly move. After that it was easier, as its course was downhill over the snow to the mouth of the pit. Glowing, and pushing, wet with perspiration, she slowly manoeuvred it along to the edge, turned it squarely, gave it a great shove and leant over anxiously. Then she gave a great sigh of relief! Just as she had hoped, it went down sharp end first and stuck fast in the snow which had saved Molly from broken bones. She was so out of breath with her work that for a moment she could not speak. Then: 'Molly, there! Now I guess you can climb up to where I can reach you.'

Molly made a rush for any way out of her prison, and climbed, like the little practised squirrel that she was, up from one stub to another to the top of the branch. She was still below the edge of the pit there, but Betsy lay flat down on the snow and held out her hands. Molly took hold hard, and, digging her toes into the snow, slowly wormed her way up to the surface of the ground.

It was then, at that very moment, that Shep came bounding up to them, barking loudly, and after him

Cousin Ann striding along in her rubber boots, with a lantern in her hand and a rather anxious look on her face.

She stopped short and looked at the two little girls, covered with snow, their faces flaming with excitement, and at the black hole gaping behind them. 'I always *told* Father we ought to put a fence around that pit,' she said in a matter-of-fact voice. 'Some day a sheep's going to fall down there. Shep came along to the house without you, and we thought most likely you'd taken the wrong turn.'

Betsy felt terribly aggrieved. She wanted to be petted and praised for her heroism. She wanted Cousin Ann to *realise* . . . Oh, if Aunt Frances were only there, *she* would realise . . . !

'I fell down in the hole, and Betsy wanted to go and get Mr Putney, but I wouldn't let her, and so she threw down a big branch and I climbed out,' explained Molly, who, now that her danger was past, took Betsy's action quite as a matter of course.

'Oh, that was how it happened,' said Cousin Ann. She looked down the hole and saw the big branch, and looked back and saw the long trail of crushed snow where Betsy had dragged it. 'Well, now, that was quite a good idea for a little girl to have,' she said briefly. 'I guess you'll do to take care of Molly all right!'

She spoke in her usual voice and immediately drew

the children after her, but Betsy's heart was singing joyfully as she trotted along clasping Cousin Ann's strong hand. Now she knew that Cousin Ann realised . . . She trotted fast, smiling to herself in the darkness.

'What made you think of doing that?' asked Cousin Ann presently, as they approached the house.

'Why, I tried to think what *you* would have done if you'd been there,' said Betsy.

'Oh!' said Cousin Ann. 'Well . . .'

She didn't say another word, but Betsy, glancing up into her face as they stepped into the lit room, saw an expression that made her give a little skip and hop of joy.

ALICE'S ADVENTURES in WONDERLAND

Lewis Carroll

Alice's adventures in Wonderland begin when she follows a white rabbit down a rabbit hole, and finds herself in a hall with many doors leading from it. She sees a beautiful garden through one tiny door but is too big to go through it. Instead she is swept away in a series of strange events, such as a Mad Hatter's tea party, where she is frustrated by the riddles and bizarre behaviour of the party guests. On her way she meets all sorts of odd people and creatures, including a caterpillar who gives her a piece of a mushroom that will make her shrink. Later she finds herself back in the hall with many doors, not knowing what odd things will happen next . . .

Once more she found herself in the long hall, and close to the little glass table. 'Now, I'll manage better this time,' she said to herself, and began by taking the little golden key, and unlocking the door that led into the garden. Then she went to work nibbling at the mushroom (she had kept a piece of it in her pocket) till she was about a foot high: then she walked down the little passage: and *then* – she found herself at last in the beautiful garden, among the bright flowerbeds and the cool fountains.

A large rose tree stood near the entrance of the garden: the roses growing on it were white, but there were three gardeners at it, busily painting them red. Alice thought this a very curious thing, and she went nearer to watch them, and just as she came up to them she heard one of them say, 'Look out now, Five! Don't go splashing paint over me like that!'

'I couldn't help it,' said Five, in a sulky tone; 'Seven jogged my elbow.'

On which Seven looked up and said, 'That's right, Five! Always lay the blame on others!'

'*You'd* better not talk!' said Five. 'I heard the Queen say only yesterday you deserved to be beheaded!'

'What for?' said the one who had spoken first.

'That's none of *your* business, Two!' said Seven.

'Yes, it *is* his business!' said Five, 'And I'll tell him – it was for bringing the cook tulip roots instead of onions.'

Seven flung down his brush, and had just begun, 'Well, of all the unjust things—' when his eye chanced to fall upon Alice, as she stood watching them, and he checked himself suddenly: the others looked round also, and all of them bowed low.

'Would you tell me,' said Alice, a little timidly, 'why you are painting those roses?'

Five and Seven said nothing, but looked at Two. Two began in a low voice, 'Why the fact is, you see, miss, this here ought to have been a *red* rose tree, and we put a white one in by mistake; and if the Queen was to find it out, we should all have our heads cut off, you know. So you see, miss, we're doing our best, afore she comes, to—' At this moment Five, who had been anxiously looking across the garden, called out, 'The Queen! The Queen!' and the three gardeners instantly threw themselves flat upon their faces. There was a sound of many footsteps, and Alice looked round, eager to see the Queen.

First came ten soldiers carrying clubs; these were all shaped like the three gardeners, oblong and flat, with their hands and feet at the corners: next the ten courtiers; these were ornamented all over with diamonds, and walked two and two, as the soldiers did. After these came the royal children; there were ten of them, and the little dears came jumping merrily along hand in hand, in couples. They were all ornamented with hearts. Next came the guests, mostly kings and queens, and among them Alice recognised the White Rabbit: it was talking in a hurried nervous manner, smiling at everything that was said, and went by without noticing her. Then followed the Knave of Hearts, carrying the King's crown on a crimson velvet cushion; and, last of all this grand procession, came THE KING AND QUEEN OF HEARTS.

Alice was rather doubtful whether she ought not to lie down on her face like the three gardeners, but she could not remember ever having heard of such a rule at processions; *And besides, what would be the use of a procession*, thought she, *if people had all to lie down upon their faces, so that they couldn't see it?* So she stood still where she was, and waited.

When the procession came opposite to Alice, they all stopped and looked at her, and the Queen said severely, 'Who is this?' She said it to the Knave of Hearts, who only bowed and smiled in reply.

'Idiot!' said the Queen, tossing her head impatiently; and, turning to Alice, she went on, 'What's your name, child?'

'My name is Alice, so please Your Majesty,' said Alice very politely; but she added, to herself, 'Why, they're only a pack of cards, after all. I needn't be afraid of them!'

'And who are *these?*' said the Queen, pointing to the three gardeners who were lying round the rose tree; for, you see, as they were lying on their faces, and the pattern on their backs was the same as the rest of the pack, she could not tell whether they were gardeners, or soldiers, or courtiers, or three of her own children.

'How should *I* know?' said Alice, surprised at her own courage. 'It's no business of *mine*.'

The Queen turned crimson with fury, and, after glaring at her for a moment like a wild beast, screamed 'Off with her head! Off—'

'Nonsense!' said Alice, very loudly and decidedly, and the Queen was silent.

The King laid his hand upon her arm, and timidly said, 'Consider, my dear: she is only a child!'

The Queen turned angrily away from him, and said to the Knave, 'Turn them over!'

The Knave did so, very carefully, with one foot.

'Get up!' said the Queen, in a shrill, loud voice, and the three gardeners instantly jumped up, and began bowing to the King, the Queen, the royal children and everybody else.

'Leave off that!' screamed the Queen. 'You make me giddy.' And then, turning to the rose tree, she went on, 'What *have* you been doing here?'

'May it please Your Majesty,' said Two, in a very humble tone, going down on one knee as he spoke, 'we were trying—'

'*I* see!' said the Queen, who had meanwhile been examining the roses. 'Off with their heads!' and the procession moved on, three of the soldiers remaining behind to execute the unfortunate gardeners, who ran to Alice for protection.

'You shan't be beheaded!' said Alice, and she put them into a large flowerpot that stood near. The three soldiers wandered about for a minute or two, looking for them, and then quietly marched off after the others.

'Are their heads off?' shouted the Queen.

'Their heads are gone, if it please Your Majesty!' the soldiers shouted in reply.

'That's right!' shouted the Queen. 'Can you play croquet?'

The soldiers were silent, and looked at Alice, as the question was evidently meant for her.

'Yes!' shouted Alice.

'Come on, then!' roared the Queen, and Alice joined the procession, wondering very much what would happen next.

The PRINCESS WHO LOVED HER FATHER LIKE SALT

Maive Stokes

This story appears in Indian Fairy Tales, *collected and translated by Maive Stokes. Stokes writes that the stories were first told to her when she was a child by two ayahs (maids or nannies) called Dunkní and Múniyá, and a servant called Karím. Like many fairy stories, different versions appear all over the world – the playwright William Shakespeare even uses a version of this tale in his tragedy* King Lear.

In a country there lived a king who had seven daughters. One day he called them all to him and said to them, 'My daughters, how much do you love me?'

The six eldest answered, 'Father, we love you as much as sweetmeats and sugar,' but the seventh and youngest daughter said, 'Father, I love you as much as salt.'

The king was much pleased with his six eldest daughters, but very angry with his youngest daughter. 'What is this?' he said. 'My daughter only loves me as much as she does salt!'

Then he called some of his servants, and said to them, 'Get a palanquin ready, and carry my youngest daughter away to the jungle.'

The servants did as they were bid; and when they got to the jungle, they put the palanquin down under a tree and went away.

The princess called to them, 'Where are you going? Stay here; my father did not tell you to leave me alone in the jungle.'

'We will come back,' said the servants, 'we are only going to drink some water.' But they returned to her father's palace.

The princess waited in the palanquin under the tree, and it was now evening, and the servants had not come back. She was very much frightened and cried bitterly. 'The tigers and wild beasts will eat me,' she said to herself. At last she went to sleep, and slept for a little while. When she awoke she found in her palanquin some food on a plate, and a little water, that God had sent her while she slept. She ate the food and drank the water, and then she felt happier, for she thought, *God must have sent me this food and water.*

She decided that as it was now night she had better stay in her palanquin, and go to sleep. *Perhaps the tigers and wild beasts will come and eat me*, she thought; *but if they don't, I will try tomorrow to get out of this jungle, and go to another country.*

The next morning she left her palanquin and set out. She walked on, till, deep in the jungle, she came to a beautiful palace, which did not belong to her father, but to another king. The gate was shut, but she opened it, and went in. She looked all about, and thought, *What a beautiful house this is, and what a pretty garden and tank!*

Everything was beautiful, only there were no servants nor anybody else to be seen. She went into the house, and through all the rooms. In one room she saw a dinner ready to be eaten, but there was no one to eat it. At last she came to a room in which was a splendid bed, and on it lay a king covered with a shawl. She took the shawl off, and then she saw he was very beautiful, and that he was dead. His body was stuck full of needles.

She sat down on the bed, and there she sat for one week, without eating, or drinking, or sleeping, pulling out the needles.

Then a man came by who said to her, 'I have here a girl I wish to sell.'

'I have no rupees,' said the princess; 'but if you will sell her to me for my gold bangles, I will buy her.'

The man took the bangles, and left the girl with the princess, who was very glad to have her. *Now*, she thought, *I shall be no longer alone.*

All day and all night long the princess sat and pulled out the needles, while the girl went about the palace doing other work. At the end of another two weeks the princess had pulled out all the needles from the king's body, except those in his eyes.

Then the king's daughter said to her servant girl, 'For three weeks I have not bathed. Get a bath ready for me, and while I am bathing sit by the king, but do not take the needles out of his eyes. I will pull them out myself.'

The servant girl promised not to pull out the needles. Then she got the bath ready; but when the king's daughter had gone to bathe, she sat down on the bed, and pulled the needles out of the king's eyes.

As soon as she had done so, he opened his eyes, and sat up. He thanked God for bringing him to life again. Then he looked about, and saw the servant girl, and said to her, 'Who has made me well and pulled all the needles out of my body?'

'I have,' she answered. Then he thanked her and said she should be his wife.

When the princess came from her bath, she found the king alive, and sitting on his bed talking to her servant. When she saw this she was very sad, but she said nothing.

The king said to the servant maid, 'Who is this girl?'

She answered, 'She is one of my servants.'

And from that moment the princess became a servant girl, and her servant girl married the king. Every day the king said, 'Can this lovely girl really be a servant? She is far more beautiful than my wife.'

One day the king thought, *I will go to another country to eat the air*. So he called the pretended princess, his wife, and told her he was going to eat the air in another country. 'What would you like me to bring you when I come back?'

She answered, 'I should like beautiful saris and clothes, and gold and silver jewels.

Then the king said, 'Call the servant girl, and ask her what she would like me to bring her.'

The real princess came, and the king said to her, 'See, I am going to another country to eat the air. What would you like me to bring for you when I return?'

'King,' she answered, 'if you can bring me what I want I will tell you what it is; but if you cannot get it, I will not tell you.'

'Tell me what it is,' said the king. 'Whatever it may be I will bring it you.'

'Good,' said the princess. 'I want a sun-jewel box.'

Now the princess knew all about the sun-jewel boxes, and that only fairies had such boxes. And she knew, too, what would be in hers if the king could get one for her, although these boxes contain sometimes one thing and sometimes another.

The king had never heard of such a box, and did not know what it was like; so he went to every country asking all the people he met what sort of box was a sun-jewel box, and where he could get it. At last one day, after a fruitless search, he was very sad, for he thought, *I have promised the servant to bring her a sun-jewel box, and now I cannot get one for her; what shall I do?*

Then he went to sleep, and had a dream. In it he saw a jungle, and in the jungle a fakir who, when he slept, slept for twelve years, and then was awake for twelve years. The king felt sure this man could give him what he wanted, so when he woke he said to his sepoys and servants, 'Stay here in this spot till I return to you; then we will go back to my country.'

He mounted his horse and set out for the jungle he had seen in his dream. He went on and on till he came to it, and there he saw the fakir lying asleep. He had been asleep for twelve years all but two weeks. Over him were a quantity of leaves, and grass, and a great deal of mud. The king began taking off all the grass, and leaves, and mud, and every day for a fortnight when he got up he cleared them all away from off the fakir.

When the fakir awoke at the end of the two weeks,

and saw that no mud, or grass, or leaves were upon him, but that he was quite clean, he was very much pleased, and said to the king, 'I have slept for twelve years, and yet I am as clean as I was when I went to sleep. When I awoke after my last sleep, I was all covered with dirt and mud, grass and leaves; but this time I am quite clean.'

The king stayed with the fakir for a week, and waited on him and did everything for him. The fakir was very much pleased with the king, and he told this to him, 'You are a very good man.' He added, 'Why did you come to this jungle? You are such a great king, what can you want from me?'

'I want a sun-jewel box,' answered the king.

'You are such a good man,' said the fakir, 'that I will give you one.'

Then the fakir went to a beautiful well, down which he went right to the bottom. There, there was a house in which lived the red fairy. She was called the red fairy not because her skin was red, for it was quite white, but because everything about her was red: her house, her clothes, and her country. She was very glad to see the fakir, and asked him why he had come to see her.

'I want you to give me a sun-jewel box,' he answered.

'Very good,' said the fairy, and she brought him one in which were seven small dolls and a little flute. 'No one but she who wants this box must open it,' said the fairy to the fakir. 'She must open it when she is quite alone and at night.' Then she told him what was in the box.

The fakir thanked her, and took the box to the king, who was delighted and made many salaams to the fakir. The fakir told him none but the person who wished for the box was to open it; but he did not tell him what more the fairy had said.

The king set off on his journey now, and when he came to his servants and sepoys, he said to them he would now return to his country, as he had found the box he wanted.

When he reached his palace he called the false princess, his wife, and gave her her silks and shawls, and scarfs, and gold and silver jewels. Then he called the servant girl – the true princess – and gave her her sun-jewel box. She took it, and was delighted to have it. She made him many salaams and went away with her box, but did not open it then, for she knew what was in it, and that she must open it at night and alone.

That night she took her box and went out all by herself to a wide plain in the jungle, and there opened it. She took the little flute, put it to her lips, and began to play, and instantly out flew the seven little dolls, who were all little fairies, and they took chairs and carpets from the box, and arranged them all in a large tent which appeared at that moment. Then the fairies bathed her, combed and rolled up her hair, put on her grand clothes and lovely slippers. But all the time the princess did nothing but cry. They brought a chair and placed it before the tent, and made her sit in it. One of them took the flute and played on it, and all the others danced before the princess, and they sang songs for her. Still she cried and cried.

At last, at four o'clock in the morning, one of the fairies said, 'Princess, why do you cry?'

'I took all the needles out of the king, all but those in his eyes,' said the princess, 'and while I was bathing, my servant girl, whom I had bought with my gold bangles, pulled these out. She told the king it was she who had pulled out all the other needles and brought him to life, and that I was her servant, and she has taken my place and is treated as the princess, and the king has married her, while I am made to do a servant's work and treated as the servant.'

'Do not cry,' said the fairies. 'Everything will be well for you by and by.'

When it was close on morning, the princess played on the flute, and all the chairs, sofas, and fairies became quite tiny and went into the box, and the tent disappeared. She shut it up, and took it back to the king's palace. The next night she again went out to the jungle plain, and all happened as on the night before.

A woodcutter was coming home late from his work, and had to pass by the plain. He wondered when he saw the tent. 'I went by some time ago,' he said to himself, 'and I saw no tent here.' He climbed up a big tree to see what was going on, and saw the fairies dancing before the princess, who sat outside the tent, and he saw how she cried though the fairies did all they could to amuse her.

Then he heard the fairies say, 'Princess, why do you cry?' And he heard her tell them how she had cured the king, and how her servant girl had taken her place and made her a servant.

'Never mind, don't cry,' said the fairies. 'All will be well by and by.'

Near morning the princess played on her flute, and the fairies went into the box, and the tent disappeared, and the princess went back to the palace.

The third night passed as the other two had done. The woodcutter came to look on, and climbed into the tree to see the fairies and the princess. Again the fairies asked her why she cried, and she gave the same answer.

The next day the woodcutter went to the king. 'Last night and the night before,' he said, 'as I came home from work, I saw a large tent in the jungle, and before the tent there sat a princess who did nothing but cry, while seven fairies danced before her, or played on different instruments, and sang songs to her.'

The king was very much astonished, and said to the woodcutter, 'Tonight I will go with you, and see the tent, and the princess, and the fairies.'

When it was night the princess went out softly and opened her box on the plain. The woodcutter fetched the king, and the two men climbed into a tree, and watched the fairies as they danced and sang. The king saw that the princess who sat and cried was his own servant girl. He heard her tell the fairies all she had done for him, and all that had happened to her; so he came suddenly down from the tree, and went up to her, and took her hand.

'I always thought you were a princess, and no servant girl,' he said. 'Will you marry me?'

She left off crying, and said, 'Yes, I will marry you.' She played on her flute, and the tent disappeared, and all the fairies, and sofas, and chairs went into the box. She put her flute in it, as she always did before shutting down the lid, and went home with the king.

The servant girl was very vexed and angry when she found the king knew all that had happened. However, the princess was most good to her, and never treated her unkindly.

The princess then sent a letter to her mother, in which she wrote, 'I am going to be married to a great king. You and my father must come to my wedding, and must bring my sisters with you.'

They all came, and her father and mother liked the king very much, and were glad their daughter should marry him. The wedding took place, and they stayed with her for some time. For a whole week she gave their servants and sepoys nice food cooked with salt, but to her father and mother and sisters she only gave food cooked with sugar. At last they got so tired of this sweet food that they could eat it no longer. At the end of the week she gave them a dinner cooked with salt.

Then her father said, 'My daughter is wise though she is so young, and is the youngest of my daughters. I know now how much she loved me when she said she loved me like salt. People cannot eat their food without salt. If their food is cooked with sugar one day, it must be cooked with salt the next, or they cannot eat it.'

After this her father and mother and sisters went home, but they often came to see their little daughter and her husband.

The princess, the king and the servant maid all lived happily together.

A LITTLE PRINCESS

Frances Hodgson Burnett

Sara Crewe is the richest girl at Miss Minchin's boarding school. Sara has a vivid imagination – she loves making up stories to entertain the other girls with, and sometimes imagines that she is a princess. She does her best to behave as a princess would, and is so kind, gracious and generous that the other girls start calling her 'Princess Sara'. But when Miss Minchin hears that Sara's father has died and left her penniless the head teacher banishes Sara to the attic of the school and makes her work as a servant alongside Becky, the scullery maid. Even here, Sara's imagination helps her to be brave as she makes up stories for Becky about the two of them being prisoners in the Bastille (a fortress in France), and invents tales about the neighbours they can see from the attic windows.

The winter was a wretched one. There were days on which Sara tramped through snow when she went on her errands; there were worse days when the snow melted and combined itself with mud to form slush; there were others when the fog was so thick that the lamps in the street were lit all day and London looked as it had looked the afternoon, several years ago, when the cab had driven through the thoroughfares with Sara tucked up on its seat, leaning against her father's shoulder. On such days the windows of the house of the Large Family always looked delightfully cosy and alluring, and the study in which the Indian gentleman sat glowed with warmth and rich colour. But the attic was dismal beyond words. There were no longer sunsets or sunrises to look at, and scarcely ever any stars, it seemed to Sara. The clouds hung low over the skylight and were either grey or mud colour, or dropping heavy rain. At four o'clock in the afternoon, even when there was no special fog, the daylight was at an end. If it was necessary to go to her attic for anything, Sara was obliged to light a candle. The women in the kitchen were depressed, and that made them more ill-tempered than ever. Becky was driven like a little slave.

"Twarn't for you, miss,' she said hoarsely to Sara one night when she had crept into the attic, "twarn't for you, an' the Bastille, an' bein' the prisoner in the next cell, I should die. That there does seem real now, doesn't it? The missus is more like the head jailer every day she lives. I can jest see them big keys you say she carries.

The cook she's like one of the under-jailers. Tell me some more, please, miss – tell me about the subt'ranean passage we've dug under the walls.'

'I'll tell you something warmer,' shivered Sara. 'Get your coverlet and wrap it round you, and I'll get mine, and we will huddle close together on the bed, and I'll tell you about the tropical forest where the Indian gentleman's monkey used to live. When I see him sitting on the table near the window and looking out into the street with that mournful expression, I always feel sure he is thinking about the tropical forest where he used to swing by his tail from coconut trees. I wonder who caught him, and if he left a family behind who had depended on him for coconuts.'

'That is warmer, miss,' said Becky, gratefully; 'but, someways, even the Bastille is sort of heatin' when you gets to tellin' about it.'

'That is because it makes you think of something else,' said Sara, wrapping the coverlet round her until only her small dark face was to be seen looking out of it. 'I've noticed this. What you have to do with your mind, when your body is miserable, is to make it think of something else.'

'Can you do it, miss?' faltered Becky, regarding her with admiring eyes.

Sara knitted her brows a moment.

'Sometimes I can and sometimes I can't,' she said stoutly. 'But when I *can* I'm all right. And what I believe is that we always could – if we practised enough. I've been practising a good deal lately, and it's beginning to be easier than it used to be. When things are horrible – just horrible – I think as hard as ever I can of being a princess. I say to myself, "I am a princess, and I am a fairy one, and because I am a fairy nothing can hurt me or make me uncomfortable." You don't know how it makes you forget,' she said with a laugh.

She had many opportunities of making her mind think of something else, and many opportunities of proving to herself whether or not she was a princess. But one of the strongest tests she was ever put to came on a certain dreadful day which, she often thought afterwards, would never quite fade out of her memory even in the years to come.

For several days it had rained continuously; the streets were chilly and sloppy and full of dreary, cold mist; there was mud everywhere – sticky London mud – and over everything the pall of drizzle and fog. Of course there were several long and tiresome errands to be done – there always were on days like this – and Sara was sent out again and again, until her shabby clothes were damp through. The absurd old feathers on her forlorn hat were more draggled and absurd than ever, and her downtrodden shoes were so wet that they could not hold any more water. Added to this, she had been deprived of her dinner, because Miss Minchin had chosen to punish her. She was so cold and hungry and tired that her face began to have a pinched look, and now and then some kind-hearted person passing her in the street glanced at her with sudden sympathy. But she did not know that. She hurried on, trying to make her mind think of something else. It was really very necessary. Her way of doing it was to 'pretend' and 'suppose' with all the strength that was left in her. But really this time it was harder than she had ever found it, and once or twice she thought it almost made her more cold and hungry instead of less so. But she persevered obstinately, and as the muddy water squelched through her broken shoes and the wind seemed trying to drag her thin jacket from her, she talked to herself as she walked, though she did not speak aloud or even move her lips.

Suppose I had dry clothes on, she thought. *Suppose I had good shoes and a long, thick coat and merino stockings and a whole umbrella. And suppose – suppose – just when I was near a baker's where they sold hot buns, I should find sixpence – which belonged to nobody. SUPPOSE if I did, I should go into the shop and buy six of the hottest buns and eat them all without stopping.*

Some very odd things happen in this world sometimes.

It certainly was an odd thing that happened to Sara. She had to cross the street just when she was saying this to herself. The mud was dreadful – she almost had to wade. She picked her way as carefully as she could, but she could not save herself much; only, in picking her way, she had to look down at her feet and the mud, and in looking down – just as she reached the pavement – she saw something shining in the gutter. It was actually a piece of silver – a tiny piece trodden upon by many feet, but still with spirit enough left to shine a little. Not quite a sixpence, but the next thing to it – a fourpenny piece.

In one second it was in her cold little red-and-blue hand.

'Oh,' she gasped, 'it is true! It is true!'

And then, if you will believe me, she looked straight at the shop directly facing her. And it was a baker's shop, and a cheerful, stout, motherly woman with rosy cheeks was putting into the window a tray of delicious newly baked hot buns, fresh from the oven – large, plump, shiny buns, with currants in them.

It almost made Sara feel faint for a few seconds – the shock, and the sight of the buns, and the delightful odours of warm bread floating up through the baker's cellar window.

She knew she need not hesitate to use the little piece

of money. It had evidently been lying in the mud for some time, and its owner was completely lost in the stream of passing people who crowded and jostled each other all day long.

'But I'll go and ask the baker woman if she has lost anything,' she said to herself, rather faintly. So she crossed the pavement and put her wet foot on the step. As she did so she saw something that made her stop.

It was a little figure more forlorn even than herself – a little figure which was not much more than a bundle of rags, from which small, bare, red muddy feet peeped out, only because the rags with which their owner was trying to cover them were not long enough. Above the rags appeared a shock head of tangled hair, and a dirty face with big, hollow, hungry eyes.

Sara knew they were hungry eyes the moment she saw them, and she felt a sudden sympathy.

'This,' she said to herself, with a little sigh, 'is one of the populace – and she is hungrier than I am.'

The child – this 'one of the populace' – stared up at Sara, and shuffled herself aside a little, so as to give her room to pass. She was used to being made to give room to everybody. She knew that if a policeman chanced to see her he would tell her to 'move on'.

Sara clutched her little fourpenny piece and hesitated for a few seconds. Then she spoke to her.

'Are you hungry?' she asked.

The child shuffled herself and her rags a little more.

'Ain't I jist?' she said in a hoarse voice. 'Jist ain't I?'

'Haven't you had any dinner?' said Sara.

'No dinner,' more hoarsely still and with more shuffling. 'Nor yet no bre'fast – nor yet no supper. No nothin'.'

'Since when?' asked Sara.

'Dunno. Never got nothin' today – nowhere. I've axed an' axed.'

Just to look at her made Sara more hungry and faint. But those queer little thoughts were at work in her brain, and she was talking to herself, though she was sick at heart.

'If I'm a princess,' she was saying, 'if I'm a princess – when they were poor and driven from their thrones – they always shared – with the populace – if they met one poorer and hungrier than themselves. They always shared. Buns are a penny each. If it had been sixpence I could have eaten six. It won't be enough for either of us. But it will be better than nothing.'

'Wait a minute,' she said to the beggar child.

She went into the shop. It was warm and smelt deliciously. The woman was just going to put some more hot buns into the window.

'If you please,' said Sara, 'have you lost fourpence – a

silver fourpence?' And she held the forlorn little piece of money out to her.

The woman looked at it and then at her – at her intense little face and draggled, once fine clothes.

'Bless us, no,' she answered. 'Did you find it?'

'Yes,' said Sara. 'In the gutter.'

'Keep it, then,' said the woman. 'It may have been there for a week, and goodness knows who lost it. *You* could never find out.'

'I know that,' said Sara, 'but I thought I would ask you.'

'Not many would,' said the woman, looking puzzled and interested and good-natured all at once.

'Do you want to buy something?' she added, as she saw Sara glance at the buns.

'Four buns, if you please,' said Sara. 'Those at a penny each.'

The woman went to the window and put some in a paper bag.

Sara noticed that she put in six.

'I said four, if you please,' she explained. 'I have only fourpence.'

'I'll throw in two for makeweight,' said the woman with her good-natured look. 'I dare say you can eat them some time. Aren't you hungry?'

A mist rose before Sara's eyes.

'Yes,' she answered. 'I am very hungry, and I am much obliged to you for your kindness; and—' She was going to add 'There is a child outside who is hungrier than I am.' But just at that moment two or three customers came in at once, and each one seemed in a hurry, so she could only thank the woman again and go out.

The beggar girl was still huddled up in the corner of the step. She looked frightful in her wet and dirty rags. She was staring straight before her with a stupid look of suffering, and Sara saw her suddenly draw the back of her roughened black hand across her eyes to rub away the tears which seemed to have surprised her by forcing their way from under her lids. She was muttering to herself.

Sara opened the paper bag and took out one of the hot buns, which had already warmed her own cold hands a little.

'See,' she said, putting the bun in the ragged lap, 'this is nice and hot. Eat it, and you will not feel so hungry.'

The child started and stared up at her, as if such sudden, amazing good luck almost frightened her; then she snatched up the bun and began to cram it into her mouth with great wolfish bites.

'Oh, my! Oh, my!' Sara heard her say hoarsely, in wild delight. 'OH my!'

Sara took out three more buns and put them down.

The sound in the hoarse, ravenous voice was awful.

'She is hungrier than I am,' she said to herself. 'She's starving.' But her hand trembled when she put down the fourth bun. 'I'm not starving,' she said – and she put down the fifth.

The little ravening London savage was still snatching and devouring when she turned away. She was too ravenous to give any thanks, even if she had ever been taught politeness – which she had not. She was only a poor little wild animal.

'Goodbye,' said Sara.

When she reached the other side of the street she looked back. The child had a bun in each hand and had stopped in the middle of a bite to watch her. Sara gave her a little nod, and the child, after another stare – a curious lingering stare – jerked her shaggy head in response, and until Sara was out of sight she did not take another bite or even finish the one she had begun.

At that moment the baker woman looked out of her shop window.

'Well, I never!' she exclaimed. 'If that young 'un hasn't given her buns to a beggar child! It wasn't because she didn't want them, either. Well, well, she looked hungry enough. I'd give something to know what she did it for.'

She stood behind her window for a few moments and

pondered. Then her curiosity got the better of her. She went to the door and spoke to the beggar child.

'Who gave you those buns?' she asked her. The child nodded her head towards Sara's vanishing figure.

'What did she say?' inquired the woman.

'Axed me if I was 'ungry,' replied the hoarse voice.

'What did you say?'

'Said I was jist.'

'And then she came in and got the buns, and gave them to you, did she?'

The child nodded.

'How many?'

'Five.'

The woman thought it over.

'Left just one for herself,' she said in a low voice. 'And she could have eaten the whole six – I saw it in her eyes.'

She looked after the little draggled far-away figure and felt more disturbed in her usually comfortable mind than she had felt for many a day.

'I wish she hadn't gone so quick,' she said. 'I'm blest if she shouldn't have had a dozen.' Then she turned to the child.

'Are you still hungry?' she said.

'I'm allus hungry,' was the answer, 'but 't ain't as bad as it was.'

'Come in here,' said the woman, and she held open the shop door.

The child got up and shuffled in. To be invited into a warm place full of bread seemed an incredible thing. She did not know what was going to happen. She did not care, even.

'Get yourself warm,' said the woman, pointing to a fire in the tiny back room. 'And look here; when you are hard up for a bit of bread, you can come in here and ask for it. I'm blest if I won't give it to you for that young one's sake.'

Sara found some comfort in her remaining bun. At all events, it was very hot, and it was better than nothing. As she walked along she broke off small pieces and ate them slowly to make them last longer.

'Suppose it was a magic bun,' she said, 'and a bite was as much as a whole dinner. I should be overeating myself if I went on like this.'

The PHOENIX
and the CARPET

E. Nesbit

The Phoenix and the Carpet *is about five children – Cyril, Anthea (nicknamed 'Panther'), Robert, Jane and their baby brother, known only by his nickname 'the Lamb' – who find a glowing egg wrapped up in the secondhand carpet that their parents have bought. When they accidentally knock the egg into the nursery fire a phoenix hatches out of it! The Phoenix tells them that the carpet is magic and can take them anywhere they wish, but can only grant three wishes each day. The children have many adventures, visiting exciting places such as a tropical island, an Indian bazaar and a French castle. They're having great fun until something goes wrong . . .*

The movement of the carpet's bright colours caught the eye of the Lamb, who went down on all fours instantly and began to pull at the red and blue threads.

'Aggedydaggedygaggedy,' murmured the Lamb; 'daggedy ag ag ag!'

And before anyone could have winked (even if they had wanted to, and it would not have been of the slightest use) the middle of the floor showed bare, an island of boards surrounded by a sea of linoleum. The magic carpet was gone, AND SO WAS THE LAMB!

There was a horrible silence. The Lamb – the baby, all alone – had been wafted away on that untrustworthy carpet, so full of holes and magic. And no one could know where he was. And no one could follow him because there was now no carpet to follow on.

Jane burst into tears, but Anthea, though pale and frantic, was dry-eyed.

'It MUST be a dream,' she said.

'That's what the clergyman said,' remarked Robert forlornly; 'but it wasn't, and it isn't.'

'But the Lamb never wished,' said Cyril; 'he was only talking Bosh.'

'The carpet understands all speech,' said the Phoenix, 'even Bosh. I know not this Boshland, but be assured that its tongue is not unknown to the carpet.'

'Do you mean, then,' said Anthea, in white terror, 'that when he was saying "Agglety dag", or whatever it was, that he meant something by it?'

'All speech has meaning,' said the Phoenix.

'There I think you're wrong,' said Cyril; 'even people who talk English sometimes say things that don't mean anything in particular.'

'Oh, never mind that now,' moaned Anthea; 'you think "Aggety dag" meant something to him and the carpet?'

'Beyond doubt it held the same meaning to the carpet as to the luckless infant,' the Phoenix said calmly.

'And WHAT did it mean? Oh WHAT?'

'Unfortunately,' the bird rejoined, 'I never studied Bosh.'

Jane sobbed noisily, but the others were calm with what is sometimes called the calmness of despair. The Lamb was gone – the Lamb, their own precious baby brother – who had never in his happy little life been for a moment out of the sight of eyes that loved him – he was gone. He had gone alone into the great world with no other companion and protector than a carpet with holes in it. The children had never really understood before what an enormously big place the world is. And the Lamb might be anywhere in it!

'And it's no use going to look for him.' Cyril, in flat and wretched tones, only said what the others were thinking.

'Do you wish him to return?' the Phoenix asked; it seemed to speak with some surprise.

'Of course we do!' cried everybody.

'Isn't he more trouble than he's worth?' asked the bird doubtfully.

'No, no. Oh, we do want him back! We do!'

'Then,' said the wearer of gold plumage, 'if you'll excuse me, I'll just pop out and see what I can do.'

Cyril flung open the window, and the Phoenix popped out.

'Oh, if only Mother goes on sleeping! Oh, suppose she wakes up and wants the Lamb! Oh, suppose the servants come! Stop crying, Jane. It's no earthly good. No, I'm not crying myself – at least I wasn't till you said so, and I shouldn't anyway if – if there was any mortal thing we could do. Oh, oh, oh!'

Cyril and Robert were boys, and boys never cry, of course. Still, the position was a terrible one, and I do not wonder that they made faces in their efforts to behave in a really manly way.

And at this awful moment Mother's bell rang.

A breathless stillness held the children. Then Anthea dried her eyes. She looked round her and caught up the poker. She held it out to Cyril.

'Hit my hand hard,' she said; 'I must show mother some reason for my eyes being like they are. Harder,' she cried as Cyril gently tapped her with the iron handle. And Cyril, agitated and trembling, nerved himself to hit harder, and hit very much harder than he intended.

Anthea screamed.

'Oh, Panther, I didn't mean to hurt, really,' cried

Cyril, clattering the poker back into the fender.

'It's – all – right,' said Anthea breathlessly, clasping the hurt hand with the one that wasn't hurt; 'it's – getting – red.'

It was – a round red and blue bump was rising on the back of it. 'Now, Robert,' she said, trying to breathe more evenly, 'you go out – oh, I don't know where – on to the dustbin – anywhere – and I shall tell Mother you and the Lamb are out.'

Anthea was now ready to deceive her mother for as long as ever she could. Deceit is very wrong, we know, but it seemed to Anthea that it was her plain duty to keep her mother from being frightened about the Lamb as long as possible. And the Phoenix might help.

'It always has helped,' Robert said; 'it got us out of the tower, and even when it made the fire in the theatre it got us out all right. I'm certain it will manage somehow.'

Mother's bell rang again.

'Oh, Eliza's never answered it,' cried Anthea; 'she never does. Oh, I must go.'

And she went.

Her heart beat bumpingly as she climbed the stairs. Mother would be certain to notice her eyes – well, her hand would account for that. But the Lamb—

'No, I must NOT think of the Lamb,' she said to herself, and bit her tongue till her eyes watered again, so as to give herself something else to think of. Her arms and legs and back, and even her tear-reddened face, felt stiff with her resolution not to let Mother be worried if she could help it.

She opened the door softly.

'Yes, Mother?' she said.

'Dearest,' said Mother, 'the Lamb—'

Anthea tried to be brave. She tried to say that the Lamb and Robert were out. Perhaps she tried too hard. Anyway, when she opened her mouth no words came. So she stood with it open. It seemed easier to keep from crying with one's mouth in that unusual position.

'The Lamb,' Mother went on; 'he was very good at first, but he's pulled the toilet cover off the dressing table with all the brushes and pots and things, and now he's so quiet I'm sure he's in some dreadful mischief. And I can't see him from here, and if I'd got out of bed to see I'm sure I should have fainted.'

'Do you mean he's HERE?' said Anthea.

'Of course he's here,' said Mother, a little impatiently. 'Where did you think he was?'

Anthea went round the foot of the big mahogany bed. There was a pause.

'He's not here NOW,' she said.

That he had been there was plain, from the toilet cover on the floor, the scattered pots and bottles, the wandering brushes and combs, all involved in the tangle of ribbons and laces which an open drawer had yielded to the baby's inquisitive fingers.

'He must have crept out, then,' said mother; 'do keep him with you, there's a darling. If I don't get some sleep I shall be a wreck when Father comes home.'

Anthea closed the door softly. Then she tore downstairs and burst into the nursery, crying, 'He must have wished he was with Mother. He's been there all the time. "Aggety dag—"'

The unusual word was frozen on her lip, as people say in books.

For there, on the floor, lay the carpet, and on the carpet, surrounded by his brothers and by Jane, sat the Lamb. He had covered his face and clothes with Vaseline and violet powder, but he was easily recognisable in spite of this disguise.

'You are right,' said the Phoenix, who was also present; 'it is evident that, as you say, "Aggety dag" is Bosh for "I want to be where my mother is", and so the faithful carpet understood it.'

'But how,' said Anthea, catching up the Lamb and hugging him, 'how did he get back here?'

'Oh,' said the Phoenix, 'I flew to the Psammead and wished that your infant brother were restored to your midst, and immediately it was so.'

'Oh, I am glad, I am glad!' cried Anthea, still hugging the baby. 'Oh, you darling! Shut up, Jane! I don't care HOW much he comes off on me! Cyril! You and Robert roll that carpet up and put it in the beetle cupboard. He might say "Aggety dag" again, and it might mean something quite different next time. Now, my Lamb, Panther'll clean you a little. Come on.'

The SEVEN RAVENS

The Brothers Grimm

This is a German fairy tale collected by two brothers, Jacob and Wilhelm Grimm, in Grimms' Fairy Tales. *Interestingly different versions of this story can be found all around the world. For example, an Italian version is called* The Seven Doves, *an Irish version is called* Twelve Wild Geese, *and a North African version is called* Udea and her Seven Brothers. *The one thing the stories have in common, however, is a brave girl who sets out on an adventure to rescue her brothers.*

There was once a man who had seven sons, and last of all one daughter. Although the little girl was very pretty, she was so weak and small that they thought she could not live; but they said she should at once be christened.

So the father sent one of his sons in haste to the spring to get some water, but the other six ran with him. Each wanted to be first at drawing the water, and so they were in such a hurry that all let their pitchers fall into the well, and they stood very foolishly looking at one another, and did not know what to do, for none dared go home. In the meantime the father was uneasy, and could not tell what made the young men stay so long. 'Surely,' said he, 'the whole seven must have forgotten themselves over some game of play'; and when he had waited still longer and they yet did not come, he flew into a rage and wished them all turned into ravens. Scarcely had he spoken these words when he heard a croaking over his head, and looked up and saw seven ravens as black as coal flying round and round. Sorry as he was to see his wish so fulfilled, he did not know how what was done could be undone, and comforted himself as well as he could for the loss of his seven sons with his dear little daughter, who soon became stronger and every day more beautiful.

For a long time she did not know that she had ever had any brothers, for her father and mother took care not to speak of them before her, but one day by chance she heard the people about her speak of them. 'Yes,' said they, 'she is beautiful indeed, but still 'tis a pity that her brothers should have been lost for her sake.' Then she was much grieved, and went to her father and mother, and asked if she had any brothers, and what had become of them. So they dared no longer hide the truth from her, but said it was the will of Heaven, and that her birth was only the innocent cause of it; but the little girl mourned sadly about it every day, and thought herself bound to do all she could to bring her brothers back; and she had neither rest nor ease, till at length one day she stole away, and set out into the wide world to find her brothers, wherever they might be, and free them, whatever it might cost her.

She took nothing with her but a little ring which her father and mother had given her, a loaf of bread in case she should be hungry, a little pitcher of water in case she should be thirsty, and a little stool to rest upon when she should be weary. Thus she went on and on, and journeyed till she came to the world's end; then she came to the sun, but the sun looked much too hot and fiery; so she ran away quickly to the moon, but the moon was cold and chilly, and said, 'I smell flesh and blood this way!' so she took herself away in a hurry and came to the stars, and the stars were friendly and kind to her, and each star sat upon his own little stool; but the morning star rose up and gave her a little piece of wood, and said, 'If you have not this little piece of wood, you cannot unlock the castle that stands on the glass mountain, and there your brothers live.' The little girl took the piece of wood, rolled it up in a little cloth, and went on again until she came to the glass mountain, and found the door shut. Then she felt for the little piece of wood; but when she unwrapped the cloth it was not there, and she saw she had lost the gift of the good stars. What was to be done? She wanted to save her brothers, and had no key of the castle of the glass mountain; so this faithful little sister took a knife out of her pocket and cut off her little finger, that was just the size of the piece of wood she had lost, and put it in the door and opened it.

As she went in, a little dwarf came up to her, and said, 'What are you seeking for?'

'I seek for my brothers, the seven ravens,' answered she.

Then the dwarf said, 'My masters are not at home; but if you will wait till they come, pray step in.' Now the little dwarf was getting their dinner ready, and he brought their food upon seven little plates, and their drink in seven little glasses, and set them upon the table, and out of each little plate their sister ate a small piece, and out of each little glass she drank a small drop; but she let the ring that she had brought with her fall into the last glass.

All of a sudden she heard a fluttering and croaking in the air, and the dwarf said, 'Here come my masters.' When they came in, they wanted to eat and drink, and looked for their little plates and glasses. Then said one after the other, 'Who has eaten from my little plate?

And who has been drinking out of my little glass?'

'Caw! Caw! Well I ween; mortal lips have this way been.'

When the seventh came to the bottom of his glass, and found there the ring, he looked at it, and knew that it was his father's and mother's, and said, 'Oh that our little sister would but come! Then we should be free.' When the little girl heard this (for she stood behind the door all the time and listened), she ran forward, and in an instant all the ravens took their right form again; and all hugged and kissed each other, and went merrily home.

POLLYANNA

Eleanor H. Porter

Orphaned Pollyanna Whittier goes to live with Aunt Polly, who does not want her. Slowly, however, Pollyanna starts to melt her aunt's stern heart with her kindness and unfailing optimism. Pollyanna becomes famous in the town as she teaches her neighbours the Glad Game, something Pollyanna and her father invented one Christmas while he was still alive. Because they were poor Pollyanna only received one Christmas present, which was donated by missionaries. She'd asked for a doll but had received a pair of crutches instead! Instead of being sad, Pollyanna decided to be glad that she didn't need to use the crutches, and so the Glad Game – the challenge of finding something to be glad about in any situation – began.

Pollyanna has one neighbour, however, who still isn't charmed by her – the bad-tempered Mr Pendleton. In the scene below Pollyanna is leaving a Ladies' Aid meeting, disappointed that none of the ladies wants to adopt her orphaned friend Jimmy Bean.

It had been a hard day, for all it had been a 'vacation one' (as she termed the infrequent days when there was no sewing or cooking lesson), and Pollyanna was sure that nothing would do her quite so much good as a walk through the green quiet of Pendleton Woods. Up Pendleton Hill, therefore, she climbed steadily, in spite of the warm sun on her back.

'I don't have to get home till half past five, anyway,' she was telling herself; 'and it'll be so much nicer to go around by the way of the woods, even if I do have to climb to get there.'

It was very beautiful in the Pendleton Woods, as Pollyanna knew by experience. But today it seemed even more delightful than ever, notwithstanding her disappointment over what she must tell Jimmy Bean tomorrow.

'I wish they were up here – all those ladies who talked so loud,' sighed Pollyanna to herself, raising her eyes to the patches of vivid blue between the sunlit green of the treetops. 'Anyhow, if they were up here, I just reckon they'd change and take Jimmy Bean for their little boy, all right,' she finished, secure in her conviction, but unable to give a reason for it, even to herself.

Suddenly Pollyanna lifted her head and listened. A dog had barked some distance ahead. A moment later he came dashing toward her, still barking.

'Hullo, doggie – hullo!' Pollyanna snapped her fingers at the dog and looked expectantly down the path. She had seen the dog once before, she was sure. He had been then with the man, Mr John Pendleton. She was looking now, hoping to see him. For some minutes she watched eagerly, but he did not appear. Then she turned her attention toward the dog.

The dog, as even Pollyanna could see, was acting strangely. He was still barking – giving little short, sharp yelps, as if of alarm. He was running back and forth, too, in the path ahead. Soon they reached a side path, and down this the little dog fairly flew, only to come back at once, whining and barking.

'Ho! That isn't the way home,' laughed Pollyanna, still keeping to the main path.

The little dog seemed frantic now. Back and forth, back and forth, between Pollyanna and the side path he vibrated, barking and whining pitifully. Every quiver of his little brown body, and every glance from his beseeching brown eyes were eloquent with appeal – so eloquent that at last Pollyanna understood, turned and followed him.

Straight ahead, now, the little dog dashed madly; and it was not long before Pollyanna came upon the reason for it all: a man lying motionless at the foot of a steep, overhanging mass of rock a few yards from the side path.

A twig cracked sharply under Pollyanna's foot, and the man turned his head. With a cry of dismay Pollyanna ran to his side.

'Mr Pendleton! Oh, are you hurt?'

'Hurt? Oh, no! I'm just taking a siesta in the sunshine,' snapped the man irritably. 'See here, how much do you know? What can you do? Have you got any sense?'

Pollyanna caught her breath with a little gasp, but – as was her habit – she answered the questions literally, one by one.

'Why, Mr Pendleton, I – I don't know so very much, and I can't do a great many things; but most of the Ladies' Aiders, except Mrs Rawson, said I had real good sense. I heard 'em say so one day – they didn't know I heard, though.'

The man smiled grimly.

'There, there, child, I beg your pardon, I'm sure; it's only this confounded leg of mine. Now listen.' He paused, and with some difficulty reached his hand into his trousers pocket and brought out a bunch of keys, singling out one between his thumb and forefinger. 'Straight through the path there, about five minutes' walk, is my house. This key will admit you to the side door under the porte-cochere. Do you know what a porte-cochere is?'

'Oh, yes, sir. Auntie has one with a sun parlour over

it. That's the roof I slept on – only I didn't sleep, you know. They found me.'

'Eh? Oh! Well, when you get into the house, go straight through the vestibule and hall to the door at the end. On the big, flat-topped desk in the middle of the room you'll find a telephone. Do you know how to use a telephone?'

'Oh, yes, sir! Why, once when Aunt Polly—'

'Never mind Aunt Polly now,' cut in the man scowlingly, as he tried to move himself a little.

'Hunt up Dr Thomas Chilton's number on the card you'll find somewhere around there – it ought to be on the hook down at the side, but it probably won't be. You know a telephone card, I suppose, when you see one!'

'Oh, yes, sir! I just love Aunt Polly's. There's such a lot of queer names, and—'

'Tell Dr Chilton that John Pendleton is at the foot of Little Eagle Ledge in Pendleton Woods with a broken leg, and to come at once with a stretcher and two men. He'll know what to do besides that. Tell him to come by the path from the house.'

'A broken leg? Oh, Mr Pendleton, how perfectly awful!' shuddered Pollyanna. 'But I'm so glad I came! Can't *I* do—'

'Yes, you can – but evidently you won't! WILL you go and do what I ask and stop talking,' moaned the man, faintly. And, with a little sobbing cry, Pollyanna went.

Pollyanna did not stop now to look up at the patches of blue between the sunlit tops of the trees. She kept her eyes on the ground to make sure that no twig nor stone tripped her hurrying feet.

It was not long before she came in sight of the house. She had seen it before, though never so near as this. She was almost frightened now at the massiveness of the great pile of grey stone with its pillared verandas and its imposing entrance. Pausing only a moment, however, she sped across the big neglected lawn and around the house to the side door under the porte-cochère. Her fingers, stiff from their tight clutch upon the keys, were anything but skilful in their efforts to turn the bolt in the lock; but at last the heavy, carved door swung slowly back on its hinges.

Pollyanna caught her breath. In spite of her feeling of haste, she paused a moment and looked fearfully through the vestibule to the wide, sombre hall beyond, her thoughts in a whirl. This was John Pendleton's house; the house of mystery; the house into which no one but its master entered; the house which sheltered, somewhere – a skeleton. Yet she, Pollyanna, was expected to enter alone these fearsome rooms, and telephone the doctor that the master of the house lay now—

With a little cry Pollyanna, looking neither to the right nor the left, fairly ran through the hall to the door at the end and opened it.

The room was large and sombre with dark woods and hangings like the hall; but through the west window the sun threw a long shaft of gold across the floor, gleamed dully on the tarnished brass andirons in the fireplace and touched the nickel of the telephone on the great desk in the middle of the room. It was toward this desk that Pollyanna hurriedly tiptoed.

The telephone card was not on its hook; it was on the floor. But Pollyanna found it, and ran her shaking forefinger down through the Cs to 'Chilton'. In due time she had Dr Chilton himself at the other end of the wires, and was tremblingly delivering her message and answering the doctor's terse, pertinent questions. This done, she hung up the receiver and drew a long breath of relief.

Only a brief glance did Pollyanna give about her; then, with a confused vision in her eyes of crimson draperies, book-lined walls, a littered floor, an untidy desk, innumerable closed doors (any one of which might conceal a skeleton) and everywhere dust, dust, dust, she fled back through the hall to the great carved door, still half open as she had left it.

In what seemed, even to the injured man, an incredibly

short time, Pollyanna was back in the woods at the man's side.

'Well, what is the trouble? Couldn't you get in?' he demanded.

Pollyanna opened wide her eyes.

'Why, of course I could! I'm HERE,' she answered. 'As if I'd be here if I hadn't got in! And the doctor will be right up just as soon as possible with the men and things. He said he knew just where you were, so I didn't stay to show him. I wanted to be with you.'

'Did you?' smiled the man, grimly. 'Well, I can't say I admire your taste. I should think you might find pleasanter companions.'

'Do you mean – because you're so – cross?'

'Thanks for your frankness. Yes.'

Pollyanna laughed softly.

'But you're only cross OUTSIDE – you arn't cross inside a bit!'

'Indeed! How do you know that?' asked the man, trying to change the position of his head without moving the rest of his body.

'Oh, lots of ways; there – like that – the way you act with the dog,' she added, pointing to the long, slender hand that rested on the dog's sleek head near him. 'It's funny how dogs and cats know the insides of folks better than other folks do, isn't it? Say, I'm going to hold your head,' she finished abruptly.

The man winced several times and groaned once, softly, while the change was being made; but in the end he found Pollyanna's lap a very welcome substitute for the rocky hollow in which his head had lain before.

'Well, that is – better,' he murmured faintly.

He did not speak again for some time. Pollyanna, watching his face, wondered if he were asleep. She did not think he was. He looked as if his lips were tight shut to keep back moans of pain. Pollyanna herself almost cried aloud as she looked at his great, strong body lying there so helpless. One hand, with fingers tightly clenched, lay outflung, motionless. The other, limply open, lay on the dog's head. The dog, his wistful, eager eyes on his master's face, was motionless, too.

Minute by minute the time passed. The sun dropped lower in the west and the shadows grew deeper under the trees. Pollyanna sat so still she hardly seemed to breathe. A bird alighted fearlessly within reach of her hand, and a squirrel whisked his bushy tail on a tree branch almost under her nose – yet with his bright little eyes all the while on the motionless dog.

At last the dog pricked up his ears and whined softly; then he gave a short, sharp bark. The next moment Pollyanna heard voices, and very soon their owners appeared: three men carrying a stretcher and various other articles.

The tallest of the party – a smooth-shaven, kind-eyed man whom Pollyanna knew by sight as Dr Chilton – advanced cheerily.

'Well, my little lady, playing nurse?'

'Oh, no, sir,' smiled Pollyanna. 'I've only held his head – I haven't given him a mite of medicine. But I'm glad I was here.'

'So am I,' nodded the doctor, as he turned his absorbed attention to the injured man.

ANNE of
GREEN GABLES

L. M. Montgomery

Marilla and Matthew Cuthbert, a middle-aged brother and sister, want to adopt a boy to help them on their farm. But the adoption agency sends a girl by mistake – Anne Shirley. After some hesitation, the Cuthberts decide to keep Anne. She is spirited, a poetry-lover and terribly accident-prone. The extract below takes place after her best friend, Diana Barry, has been banned from spending time with Anne after the girls accidentally got drunk on currant wine, thinking it was harmless raspberry cordial.

Just as Anne emerged triumphantly from the cellar with her plateful of russets came the sound of flying footsteps on the icy boardwalk outside and the next moment the kitchen door was flung open and in rushed Diana Barry, white-faced and breathless, with a shawl wrapped hastily around her head. Anne promptly let go of her candle and plate in her surprise, and plate, candle and apples crashed together down the cellar ladder and were found at the bottom embedded in melted grease, the next day, by Marilla, who gathered them up and thanked mercy the house hadn't been set on fire.

'Whatever is the matter, Diana?' cried Anne. 'Has your mother relented at last?'

'Oh, Anne, do come quick,' implored Diana nervously. 'Minnie May is awful sick – she's got croup. Young Mary Joe says – and Father and Mother are away to town and there's nobody to go for the doctor. Minnie May is awful bad and Young Mary Joe doesn't know what to do – and oh, Anne, I'm so scared!'

Matthew, without a word, reached out for cap and coat, slipped past Diana and away into the darkness of the yard.

'He's gone to harness the sorrel mare to go to Carmody for the doctor,' said Anne, who was hurrying on hood and jacket. 'I know it as well as if he'd said so. Matthew and I are such kindred spirits I can read his thoughts without words at all.'

'I don't believe he'll find the doctor at Carmody,' sobbed Diana. 'I know that Dr Blair went to town and I guess Dr Spencer would go too. Young Mary Joe never saw anybody with croup and Mrs Lynde is away. Oh, Anne!'

'Don't cry, Di,' said Anne cheerily. 'I know exactly

what to do for croup. You forget that Mrs Hammond had twins three times. When you look after three pairs of twins you naturally get a lot of experience. They all had croup regularly. Just wait till I get the ipecac bottle – you mayn't have any at your house. Come on now.'

The two little girls hastened out hand in hand and hurried through Lover's Lane and across the crusted field beyond, for the snow was too deep to go by the shorter wood way. Anne, although sincerely sorry for Minnie May, was far from being insensible to the romance of the situation and to the sweetness of once more sharing that romance with a kindred spirit.

The night was clear and frosty, all ebony of shadow and silver of snowy slope; big stars were shining over the silent fields; here and there the dark pointed firs stood up with snow powdering their branches and the wind whistling through them. Anne thought it was truly delightful to go skimming through all this mystery and loveliness with your bosom friend who had been so long estranged.

Minnie May, aged three, was really very sick. She lay on the kitchen sofa feverish and restless, while her hoarse breathing could be heard all over the house. Young Mary Joe, a buxom, broad-faced French girl from the creek, whom Mrs Barry had engaged to stay with the children during her absence, was helpless and bewildered, quite incapable of thinking what to do, or doing it if she thought of it.

Anne went to work with skill and promptness.

'Minnie May has croup all right; she's pretty bad, but I've seen them worse. First we must have lots of hot water. I declare, Diana, there isn't more than a cupful in the kettle! There, I've filled it up, and, Mary Joe, you may put some wood in the stove. I don't want to hurt your feelings but it seems to me you might have thought of this before if you'd any imagination. Now, I'll undress Minnie May and put her to bed and you try to find some soft flannel cloths, Diana. I'm going to give her a dose of ipecac first of all.'

Minnie May did not take kindly to the ipecac but Anne had not brought up three pairs of twins for nothing. Down that ipecac went, not only once, but many times during the long, anxious night when the two little girls worked patiently over the suffering Minnie May, and Young Mary Joe, honestly anxious to do all she could, kept up a roaring fire and heated more water than would have been needed for a hospital of croupy babies.

It was three o'clock when Matthew came with a doctor, for he had been obliged to go all the way to Spencervale for one. But the pressing need for assistance was past. Minnie May was much better and was sleeping soundly.

'I was awfully near giving up in despair,' explained Anne. 'She got worse and worse until she was sicker than ever the Hammond twins were, even the last pair. I actually thought she was going to choke to death. I gave her every drop of ipecac in that bottle and when the last dose went down I said to myself – not to Diana or Young Mary Joe, because I didn't want to worry them any more than they were worried, but I had to say it to myself just to relieve my feelings. "This is the last lingering hope and I fear, 'tis a vain one." But in about three minutes she coughed up the phlegm and began to get better right away. You must just imagine my relief, doctor, because I can't express it in words. You know there are some things that cannot be expressed in words.'

'Yes, I know,' nodded the doctor. He looked at Anne as if he were thinking some things about her that couldn't be expressed in words. Later on, however, he expressed them to Mr and Mrs Barry.

'That little red-headed girl they have over at Cuthberts' is as smart as they make 'em. I tell you she saved that baby's life, for it would have been too late by the time I got there. She seems to have a skill and presence of mind perfectly wonderful in a child of her age. I never saw anything like the eyes of her when she was explaining the case to me.'

Anne had gone home in the wonderful, white-frosted

winter morning, heavy-eyed from loss of sleep, but still talking unweariedly to Matthew as they crossed the long white field and walked under the glittering fairy arch of the Lover's Lane maples.

'Oh, Matthew, isn't it a wonderful morning? The world looks like something God had just imagined for His own pleasure, doesn't it? Those trees look as if I could blow them away with a breath – pouf! I'm so glad I live in a world where there are white frosts, aren't you? And I'm so glad Mrs Hammond had three pairs of twins after all. If she hadn't I mightn't have known what to do for Minnie May. I'm real sorry I was ever cross with Mrs Hammond for having twins. But, oh, Matthew, I'm so sleepy. I can't go to school. I just know I couldn't keep my eyes open and I'd be so stupid. But I hate to stay home, for Gil – some of the others will get head of the class, and it's so hard to get up again – although of course the harder it is the more satisfaction you have when you do get up, haven't you?'

'Well now, I guess you'll manage all right,' said Matthew, looking at Anne's white little face and the dark shadows under her eyes. 'You just go right to bed and have a good sleep. I'll do all the chores.'

Anne accordingly went to bed and slept so long and soundly that it was well on in the white and rosy winter afternoon when she awoke and descended to the kitchen where Marilla, who had arrived home in the meantime, was sitting knitting.

'Oh, did you see the Premier?' exclaimed Anne at once. 'What did he look like, Marilla?'

'Well, he never got to be Premier on account of his looks,' said Marilla. 'Such a nose as that man had! But he can speak. I was proud of being a Conservative. Rachel Lynde, of course, being a Liberal, had no use for him. Your dinner is in the oven, Anne, and you can get yourself some blue plum preserve out of the pantry. I guess you're hungry. Matthew has been telling me about last night. I must say it was fortunate you knew what to do. I wouldn't have had any idea myself, for I never saw a case of croup. There now, never mind talking till you've had your dinner. I can tell by the look of you that you're just full up with speeches, but they'll keep.'

Marilla had something to tell Anne, but she did not tell it just then for she knew if she did Anne's consequent excitement would lift her clear out of the region of such material matters as appetite or dinner.

Not until Anne had finished her saucer of blue plums did Marilla say, 'Mrs Barry was here this afternoon, Anne. She wanted to see you, but I wouldn't wake you up. She says you saved Minnie May's life, and she is very sorry she acted as she did in that affair of the currant wine. She says she knows now you didn't mean to set Diana drunk, and she hopes you'll forgive her and be good friends with Diana again. You're to go over this evening if you like for Diana can't stir outside the door on account of a bad cold she caught last night. Now, Anne Shirley, for pity's sake don't fly up into the air.'

The warning seemed not unnecessary, so uplifted and aerial was Anne's expression and attitude as she sprang to her feet, her face irradiated with the flame of her spirit.

'Oh, Marilla, can I go right now – without washing my dishes? I'll wash them when I come back, but I cannot tie myself down to anything so unromantic as dishwashing at this thrilling moment.'

'Yes, yes, run along,' said Marilla indulgently. 'Anne Shirley – are you crazy? Come back this instant and put something on you. I might as well call to the wind. She's gone without a cap or wrap. Look at her tearing through the orchard with her hair streaming. It'll be a mercy if she doesn't catch her death of cold.'

Anne came dancing home in the purple winter twilight across the snowy places. Afar in the south-west was the great shimmering, pearl-like sparkle of an evening star in a sky that was pale golden and ethereal rose over gleaming white spaces and dark glens of spruce. The tinkles of sleigh bells among the snowy hills came like elfin chimes through the frosty air, but their music was not sweeter than the song in Anne's heart and on her lips.

'You see before you a perfectly happy person, Marilla,' she announced. 'I'm perfectly happy – yes, in spite of my red hair. Just at present I have a soul above red hair. Mrs Barry kissed me and cried and said she was so sorry and she could never repay me. I felt fearfully embarrassed, Marilla, but I just said as politely as I could, "I have no hard feelings for you, Mrs Barry. I assure you once for all that I did not mean to intoxicate Diana and henceforth I shall cover the past with the mantle of oblivion." That was a pretty dignified way of speaking, wasn't it, Marilla?

'I felt that I was heaping coals of fire on Mrs Barry's head. And Diana and I had a lovely afternoon. Diana showed me a new fancy crochet stitch her aunt over at Carmody taught her. Not a soul in Avonlea knows it but us, and we pledged a solemn vow never to reveal it to anyone else. Diana gave me a beautiful card with a wreath of roses on it and a verse of poetry:

'*If you love me as I love you*
Nothing but death can part us two.'

'And that is true, Marilla. We're going to ask Mr Phillips to let us sit together in school again, and Gertie Pye can go with Minnie Andrews. We had an elegant tea. Mrs Barry had the very best china set out, Marilla, just as if I was real company. I can't tell you what a thrill it gave me. Nobody ever used their very best china on my account before. And we had fruit cake and pound cake and doughnuts and two kinds of preserves, Marilla. And Mrs Barry asked me if I took tea and said, "Pa, why don't you pass the biscuits to Anne?" It must be lovely to be grown up, Marilla, when just being treated as if you were is so nice.'

'I don't know about that,' said Marilla, with a brief sigh.

'Well, anyway, when I am grown up,' said Anne decidedly, 'I'm always going to talk to little girls as if they were too, and I'll never laugh when they use big words. I know from sorrowful experience how that hurts one's feelings. After tea Diana and I made taffy. The taffy wasn't very good, I suppose because neither Diana nor I had ever made any before. Diana left me to stir it while she buttered the plates and I forgot and let it burn; and then when we set it out on the platform to cool the cat walked over one plate and that had to be thrown away. But the making of it was splendid fun. Then when I came home Mrs Barry asked me to come over as often as I could and Diana stood at the window and threw kisses to me all the way down to Lover's Lane. I assure you, Marilla, that I feel like praying tonight and I'm going to think out a special brand-new prayer in honour of the occasion.'

The
POMEGRANATE SEEDS

Nathaniel Hawthorne

The story of Proserpina – or Persephone, as she is sometimes called – is an ancient Greek myth, retold here by Nathaniel Hawthorne in a collection called Tanglewood Tales for Boys and Girls. *One day, while Proserpina is picking flowers, she is kidnapped by the god of the Underworld, King Pluto, who thinks she will cheer up his gloomy palace. Proserpina bravely tells Pluto that she will not eat or drink anything until he lets her return home to her mother. Because she misses her daughter Mother Ceres casts a spell so that spring won't come until Proserpina reappears.*

The child had declared, as you may remember, that she would not taste a mouthful of food as long as she should be compelled to remain in King Pluto's palace. How she contrived to maintain her resolution, and at the same time to keep herself tolerably plump and rosy, is more than I can explain; but some young ladies, I am given to understand, possess the faculty of living on air, and Proserpina seems to have possessed it too. At any rate, it was now six months since she left the outside of the earth; and not a morsel, so far as the attendants were able to testify, had yet passed between her teeth. This was the more creditable to Proserpina, inasmuch as King Pluto had caused her to be tempted day after day, with all manner of sweetmeats, and richly preserved fruits, and delicacies of every sort, such as young people are generally most fond of. But her good mother had often told her of the hurtfulness of these things; and for that reason alone, if there had been no other, she would have resolutely refused to taste them.

All this time, being of a cheerful and active disposition, the little damsel was not quite so unhappy as you may have supposed. The immense palace had a thousand rooms, and was full of beautiful and wonderful objects. There was a never-ceasing gloom, it is true, which half hid itself among the innumerable pillars, gliding before the child as she wandered among them, and treading stealthily behind her in the echo of her footsteps. Neither was all the dazzle of the precious stones, which flamed with their own light, worth one gleam of natural sunshine; nor could the most brilliant of the many-coloured gems, which Proserpina had for playthings, vie with the simple beauty of the flowers she used to gather. But still, wherever the girl went, among those gilded halls and chambers, it seemed as if she carried nature and sunshine along with her, and as if she scattered dewy blossoms on her right hand and on her left. After Proserpina came, the palace was no longer the same abode of stately artifice and dismal magnificence that it had before been. The inhabitants all felt this, and King Pluto more than any of them.

'My own little Proserpina,' he used to say, 'I wish you could like me a little better. We gloomy and cloudy-natured persons have often as warm hearts at bottom, as those of a more cheerful character. If you would only stay with me of your own accord, it would make me happier than the possession of a hundred such palaces as this.'

'Ah,' said Proserpina, 'you should have tried to make me like you before carrying me off. And the best thing you can do now is to let me go again. Then I might remember you sometimes, and think that you were as kind as you knew how to be. Perhaps, too, one day or other, I might come back, and pay you a visit.'

'No, no,' answered Pluto, with his gloomy smile, 'I will not trust you for that. You are too fond of living in the broad daylight, and gathering flowers. What an idle and childish taste that is! Are not these gems, which I have ordered to be dug for you, and which are richer than any in my crown – are they not prettier than a violet?'

'Not half so pretty,' said Proserpina, snatching the gems from Pluto's hand, and flinging them to the other end of the hall. 'Oh, my sweet violets, shall I never see you again?'

And then she burst into tears. But young people's tears have very little saltiness or acidity in them, and do not inflame the eyes so much as those of grown persons; so that it is not to be wondered at if, a few moments afterwards, Proserpina was sporting through the hall almost as merrily as she and the four sea nymphs had sported along the edge of the surf wave. King Pluto gazed after her, and wished that he, too, was a child. And little Proserpina, when she turned about, and beheld this great king standing in his splendid hall, and looking so grand, and so melancholy, and so lonesome, was smitten with a kind of pity. She ran back to him, and, for the first time in all her life, put her small soft hand in his.

'I love you a little,' whispered she, looking up in his face.

'Do you, indeed, my dear child?' cried Pluto, bending his dark face down to kiss her; but Proserpina shrank away from the kiss, for though his features were noble, they were very dusky and grim. 'Well, I have not deserved it of you, after keeping you a prisoner for so many months, and starving you, besides. Are you not terribly hungry? Is there nothing which I can get you to eat?'

In asking this question, the king of the mines had a very cunning purpose; for, you will recollect, if Proserpina tasted a morsel of food in his dominions, she would never afterwards be at liberty to quit them.

'No, indeed,' said Proserpina. 'Your head cook is always baking, and stewing, and roasting, and rolling out paste, and contriving one dish or another, which he imagines may be to my liking. But he might just as well save himself the trouble, poor, fat little man that he is. I have no appetite for anything in the world, unless it were a slice of bread of my mother's own baking, or a little fruit out of her garden.'

When Pluto heard this, he began to see that he had mistaken the best method of tempting Proserpina to eat. The cook's dishes and artificial dainties were not half so delicious, in the good child's opinion, as the simple fare to which Mother Ceres had accustomed her. Wondering that he had never thought of it before, the king now sent one of his trusty attendants, with a large basket, to get some of the finest and juiciest pears, peaches and plums which could anywhere be found in the upper world. Unfortunately, however, this was during the time when

Ceres had forbidden any fruits or vegetables to grow; and, after seeking all over the earth, King Pluto's servant found only a single pomegranate, and that so dried up as to be not worth eating. Nevertheless, since there was no better to be had, he brought this dry, old, withered pomegranate home to the palace, put it on a magnificent golden salver, and carried it up to Proserpina. Now it happened, curiously enough, that, just as the servant was bringing the pomegranate into the back door of the palace, our friend Quicksilver had gone up the front steps, on his errand to get Proserpina away from King Pluto.

As soon as Proserpina saw the pomegranate on the golden salver, she told the servant he had better take it away again.

'I shall not touch it, I assure you,' said she. 'If I were ever so hungry, I should never think of eating such a miserable, dry pomegranate as that.'

'It is the only one in the world,' said the servant.

He set down the golden salver, with the wizened pomegranate upon it, and left the room. When he was gone, Proserpina could not help coming close to the table, and looking at this poor specimen of dried fruit with a great deal of eagerness; for, to say the truth, on seeing something that suited her taste, she felt all the six months' appetite taking possession of her at once. To be sure, it was a very wretched-looking pomegranate, and seemed to have no more juice in it than an oyster-shell. But there was no choice of such things in King Pluto's palace. This was the first fruit she had seen there, and the last she was ever likely to see; and unless she ate it up immediately, it would grow drier than it already was, and be wholly unfit to eat.

At least, I may smell it, thought Proserpina.

So she took up the pomegranate, and applied it to her nose; and, somehow or other, being in such close neighbourhood to her mouth, the fruit found its way into that little red cave. Dear me! What an everlasting pity! Before Proserpina knew what she was about, her teeth had actually bitten it, of their own accord. Just as this fatal deed was done, the door of the apartment opened, and in came King Pluto, followed by Quicksilver, who had been urging him to let his little prisoner go. At the first noise of their entrance, Proserpina withdrew the pomegranate from her mouth. But Quicksilver (whose eyes were very keen, and his wits the sharpest that ever anybody had) perceived that the child was a little confused; and seeing the empty salver, he suspected that she had been taking a sly nibble of something or other. As for honest Pluto, he never guessed at the secret.

'My little Proserpina,' said the king, sitting down, and affectionately drawing her between his knees, 'here is Quicksilver, who tells me that a great many misfortunes have befallen innocent people on account of my detaining you in my dominions. To confess the truth, I myself had already reflected that it was an unjustifiable act to take you away from your good mother. But, then, you must consider, my dear child, that this vast palace is apt to be gloomy (although the precious stones certainly shine very bright), and that I am not of the most cheerful disposition, and that therefore it was a natural thing enough to seek for the society of some merrier creature than myself. I hoped you would take my crown for a plaything, and me – ah, you laugh, naughty Proserpina – me, grim as I am, for a playmate. It was a silly expectation.'

'Not so extremely silly,' whispered Proserpina. 'You have really amused me very much, sometimes.'

'Thank you,' said King Pluto, rather dryly. 'But I can see, plainly enough, that you think my palace a dusky prison, and me the iron-hearted keeper of it. And an iron heart I should surely have, if I could detain you here any longer, my poor child, when it is now six months since you tasted food. I give you your liberty. Go with Quicksilver. Hasten home to your dear mother.'

Now, although you may not have supposed it, Proserpina found it impossible to take leave of poor King Pluto without some regrets, and a good deal of compunction for not telling him about the pomegranate. She even shed a tear or two, thinking how lonely and cheerless the great palace would seem to him, with all its ugly glare of artificial light, after she herself – his one little ray of natural sunshine, whom he had stolen, to be sure, but only because he valued her so much – after she should have departed. I know not how many kind things she might have said to the disconsolate king of the mines, had not Quicksilver hurried her away.

'Come along quickly,' whispered he in her ear, 'or His Majesty may change his royal mind. And take care, above all things, that you say nothing of what was brought you on the golden salver.'

In a very short time, they had passed the great gateway (leaving the three-headed Cerberus, barking, and yelping, and growling, with threefold din, behind them), and emerged upon the surface of the earth. It was delightful to behold, as Proserpina hastened along, how the path grew verdant behind and on either side of her. Wherever she set her blessed foot, there was at once a dewy flower. The violets gushed up along the wayside. The grass and the grain began to sprout with tenfold vigour and luxuriance, to make up for the dreary months that had been wasted in barrenness. The starved cattle immediately set to work grazing, after their long fast, and ate enormously all day, and got up at midnight to eat more. But I can assure you it was a busy time of year with the farmers, when they found the summer coming upon them with such a rush. Nor must I forget to say that all the birds in the whole world hopped about upon the newly blossoming trees, and sang together in a prodigious ecstasy of joy.

Mother Ceres had returned to her deserted home, and was sitting disconsolately on the doorstep, with her torch burning in her hand. She had been idly watching the flame for some moments past, when, all at once, it flickered and went out.

What does this mean? thought she. *It was an enchanted torch, and should have kept burning till my child came back.*

Lifting her eyes, she was surprised to see a sudden verdure flashing over the brown and barren fields, exactly as you may have observed a golden hue gleaming far and wide across the landscape, from the just risen sun.

'Does the earth disobey me?' exclaimed Mother Ceres, indignantly. 'Does it presume to be green, when I have bidden it be barren, until my daughter shall be restored to my arms?'

'Then open your arms, dear mother,' cried a well-known voice, 'and take your little daughter into them.'

And Proserpina came running, and flung herself upon her mother's bosom. Their mutual transport is not to be described. The grief of their separation had caused both of them to shed a great many tears; and now they shed a great many more, because their joy could not so well express itself in any other way.

When their hearts had grown a little more quiet, Mother Ceres looked anxiously at Proserpina.

'My child,' said she, 'did you taste any food while you were in King Pluto's palace?'

'Dearest mother,' answered Proserpina, 'I will tell you the whole truth. Until this very morning, not a morsel of food had passed my lips. But today, they brought me a pomegranate (a very dry one it was, and all shrivelled up, till there was little left of it but seeds and skin), and having seen no fruit for so long a time, and being faint with hunger, I was tempted just to bite it. The instant I tasted it, King Pluto and Quicksilver came into the room. I had not swallowed a morsel; but – dear mother, I hope it was no harm – but six of the pomegranate seeds, I am afraid, remained in my mouth.'

'Ah, unfortunate child, and miserable me!' exclaimed Ceres. 'For each of those six pomegranate seeds you must spend one month of every year in King Pluto's palace. You are but half restored to your mother. Only six months with me, and six with that good-for-nothing King of Darkness!'

'Do not speak so harshly of poor King Pluto,' said

Proserpina, kissing her mother. 'He has some very good qualities; and I really think I can bear to spend six months in his palace, if he will only let me spend the other six with you. He certainly did very wrong to carry me off; but then, as he says, it was but a dismal sort of life for him, to live in that great gloomy place, all alone; and it has made a wonderful change in his spirits to have a little girl to run upstairs and down. There is some comfort in making him so happy; and so, upon the whole, dearest mother, let us be thankful that he is not to keep me the whole year round.'

WUTHERING HEIGHTS

Emily Brontë

Emily Brontë is the sister of Charlotte Brontë, whose Jane Eyre *appears earlier in this book. When Charlotte, Emily and their younger sister, Anne, were first published, they thought they would not be taken seriously as women, so they pretended to be men! Charlotte's pen-name was Currer Bell, Emily's was Ellis Bell and Anne's was Acton Bell.*

Wuthering Heights is the name of the house on the wild Yorkshire moors where Cathy Earnshaw and her adopted brother, Heathcliff, live. In the extract below their father has recently died and their older brother, Hindley Earnshaw, is now the master of the house. Hindley hates Heathcliff and makes him live as a servant instead of a member of the family. The narrator here is Nelly Dean, the housekeeper.

Heathcliff bore his degradation pretty well at first, because Cathy taught him what she learnt, and worked or played with him in the fields. They both promised fair to grow up as rude as savages; the young master being entirely negligent how they behaved, and what they did, so they kept clear of him. He would not even have seen after their going to church on Sundays, only Joseph and the curate reprimanded his carelessness when they absented themselves; and that reminded him to order Heathcliff a flogging, and Catherine a fast from dinner or supper. But it was one of their chief amusements to run away to the moors in the morning and remain there all day, and the after punishment grew a mere thing to laugh at. The curate might set as many chapters as he pleased for Catherine to get by heart, and Joseph might thrash Heathcliff till his arm ached; they forgot everything the minute they were together again: at least the minute they had contrived some naughty plan of revenge; and many a time I've cried to myself to watch them growing more reckless daily, and I not daring to speak a syllable, for fear of losing the small power I still retained over the unfriended creatures. One Sunday evening, it chanced that they were banished from the sitting room, for making a noise, or a light offence of the kind; and when I went to call them to supper, I could discover them nowhere. We searched the house, above and below, and the yard and stables; they were invisible: and, at last, Hindley in a passion told us to bolt the doors and swore nobody should let them in that night.

The household went to bed; and I, too, anxious to lie down, opened my lattice and put my head out to hearken, though it rained: determined to admit them in spite of the prohibition, should they return. In a while, I distinguished steps coming up the road, and the light of a lantern glimmered through the gate. I threw a shawl over my head and ran to prevent them from waking Mr Earnshaw by knocking. There was Heathcliff, by himself: it gave me a start to see him alone.

'Where is Miss Catherine?' I cried hurriedly. 'No accident, I hope?'

'At Thrushcross Grange,' he answered; 'and I would have been there too, but they had not the manners to ask me to stay.'

'Well, you will catch it!' I said, 'You'll never be content till you're sent about your business. What in the world led you wandering to Thrushcross Grange?'

'Let me get off my wet clothes, and I'll tell you all about it, Nelly,' he replied. I bid him beware of rousing the master, and while he undressed and I waited to put out the candle, he continued. 'Cathy and I escaped from the washhouse to have a ramble at liberty, and getting a glimpse of the Grange lights, we thought we would just go and see whether the Lintons passed their Sunday evenings standing shivering in corners, while their father and mother sat eating and drinking, and singing and laughing, and burning their eyes out before the fire. Do you think they do? Or reading sermons, and being catechised by their manservant, and set to learn a column of Scripture names, if they don't answer properly?'

'Probably not,' I responded. 'They are good children, no doubt, and don't deserve the treatment you receive, for your bad conduct.'

'Don't cant, Nelly,' he said, 'nonsense! We ran from the top of the Heights to the park, without stopping – Catherine completely beaten in the race, because she was barefoot. You'll have to seek for her shoes in the bog tomorrow. We crept through a broken hedge, groped our way up the path, and planted ourselves on a flower-plot under the drawing-room window. The light came from thence; they had not put up the shutters, and the curtains were only half closed. Both of us were able to look in by standing on the basement, and clinging to the ledge, and we saw – ah! it was beautiful – a splendid place carpeted with crimson, and crimson-covered chairs and tables, and a pure white ceiling bordered by gold, a shower of glass drops hanging in silver chains from the centre, and shimmering with little soft tapers. Old Mr and Mrs Linton were not there; Edgar and his sisters had it entirely to themselves. Shouldn't they have been happy? We should have thought ourselves in heaven! And now, guess what your good children were doing?

Isabella – I believe she is eleven, a year younger than Cathy – lay screaming at the further end of the room, shrieking as if witches were running red-hot needles into her. Edgar stood on the hearth weeping silently, and in the middle of the table sat a little dog, shaking its paw and yelping; which, from their mutual accusations, we understood they had nearly pulled in two between them. The idiots! That was their pleasure! To quarrel who should hold a heap of warm hair, and each begin to cry because both, after struggling to get it, refused to take it. We laughed outright at the petted things; we did despise them! When would you catch me wishing to have what Catherine wanted? Or find us by ourselves, seeking entertainment in yelling, and sobbing, and rolling on the ground, divided by the whole room? I'd not exchange, for a thousand lives, my condition here, for Edgar Linton's at Thrushcross Grange – not if I might have the privilege of flinging Joseph off the highest gable, and painting the house front with Hindley's blood!'

'Hush, hush!' I interrupted. 'Still you have not told me, Heathcliff, how Catherine is left behind?'

'I told you we laughed,' he answered. 'The Lintons heard us, and with one accord they shot like arrows to the door; there was silence, and then a cry, "Oh, Mamma, Mamma! Oh, Papa! Oh, Mamma, come here. Oh, Papa, oh!" They really did howl out something in that way. We made frightful noises to terrify them still more, and then we dropped off the ledge, because somebody was drawing the bars, and we felt we had better flee. I had Cathy by the hand, and was urging her on, when all at once she fell down. "Run, Heathcliff, run!" she whispered. "They have let the bulldog loose, and he holds me!" The devil had seized her ankle, Nelly: I heard his abominable snorting. She did not yell out – no! She would have scorned to do it, if she had been spitted on the horns of a mad cow. I did, though: I vociferated curses enough to annihilate any fiend in Christendom; and I got a stone and thrust it between his jaws, and tried with all my might to cram it down his throat. A beast of a servant came up with a lantern, at last, shouting – "Keep fast, Skulker, keep fast!" He changed his note, however, when he saw Skulker's game. The dog was throttled off; his huge, purple tongue hanging half a foot out of his mouth, and his pendent lips streaming with bloody slaver. The man took Cathy up; she was sick: not from fear, I'm certain, but from pain.

'He carried her in; I followed, grumbling execrations and vengeance. "What prey, Robert?" hallooed Linton from the entrance. "Skulker has caught a little girl, sir," he replied; "and there's a lad here," he added, making a clutch at me, "who looks an out-and-outer! Very like the robbers were for putting them through the window to open the doors to the gang after all were asleep, that they might murder us at their ease. Hold your tongue, you foul-mouthed thief, you! You shall go to the gallows for this. Mr Linton, sir, don't lay by your gun."

'"No, no, Robert," said the old fool. "The rascals knew that yesterday was my rent day: they thought to have me cleverly. Come in; I'll furnish them a reception. There, John, fasten the chain. Give Skulker some water, Jenny. To beard a magistrate in his stronghold, and on the Sabbath, too! Where will their insolence stop? Oh, my dear Mary, look here! Don't be afraid, it is but a boy – yet the villain scowls so plainly in his face; would it not be a kindness to the country to hang him at once, before he shows his nature in acts as well as features?" He pulled me under the chandelier, and Mrs Linton placed her spectacles on her nose and raised her hands in horror. The cowardly children crept nearer also, Isabella lisping – "Frightful thing! Put him in the cellar, Papa. He's exactly like the son of the fortune-teller that stole my tame pheasant. Isn't he, Edgar?"

'While they examined me, Cathy came round; she heard the last speech, and laughed. Edgar Linton, after an inquisitive stare, collected sufficient wit to recognise her. They see us at church, you know, though we seldom meet them elsewhere. "That's Miss Earnshaw," he whispered to his mother, "and look how Skulker has bitten her – how her foot bleeds!"

'"Miss Earnshaw? Nonsense!" cried the dame; "Miss Earnshaw scouring the country with a gipsy! And yet, my dear, the child is in mourning – surely it is – and she may be lamed for life!"

'"What culpable carelessness in her brother!" exclaimed Mr Linton, turning from me to Catherine. "I've understood from Shielders"' (that was the curate, sir) '"that he lets her grow up in absolute heathenism. But who is this? Where did she pick up this companion? Oho! I declare he is that strange acquisition my late neighbour made, in his journey to Liverpool – a little Lascar, or an American or Spanish castaway."

'"A wicked boy, at all events," remarked the old lady, "and quite unfit for a decent house! Did you notice his language, Linton? I'm shocked that my children should have heard it."

'I recommenced cursing – don't be angry, Nelly – and so Robert was ordered to take me off. I refused to go without Cathy; he dragged me into the garden, pushed the lantern into my hand, assured me that Mr Earnshaw should be informed of my behaviour, and, bidding me march directly, secured the door again. The curtains were still looped up at one corner, and I resumed my station as spy; because, if Catherine had wished to return, I intended shattering their great glass panes to a million fragments, unless they let her out. She sat on the sofa quietly. Mrs Linton took off the grey cloak of the dairy-maid which we had borrowed for our excursion, shaking her head and expostulating with her, I suppose: she was a young lady, and they made a distinction between her treatment and mine. Then the woman servant brought a basin of warm water, and washed her feet; and Mr Linton mixed a tumbler of negus, and Isabella emptied a plateful of cakes into her lap, and Edgar stood gaping at a distance. Afterwards, they dried and combed her beautiful hair, and gave her a pair of enormous slippers, and wheeled her to the fire; and I left her, as merry as she could be, dividing her food between the little dog and Skulker, whose nose she pinched as he ate; and kindling a spark of spirit in the vacant blue eyes of the Lintons – a dim reflection from her own enchanting face. I saw they were full of stupid admiration; she is so immeasurably superior to them – to everybody on earth, is she not, Nelly?'

'There will more come of this business than you reckon on,' I answered, covering him up and extinguishing the light. 'You are incurable, Heathcliff; and Mr Hindley will have to proceed to extremities, see if he won't.'

EMILY of
NEW MOON

L. M. Montgomery

When Emily Starr's beloved father dies, making her an orphan, her aunts and uncles can't decide what to do with her. None of them want her, so they all write their names on slips of paper and ask Emily to take one without looking. She chooses proud Aunt Elizabeth, who lives with gentle Aunt Laura and kind Uncle Jimmy on New Moon Farm. Despite this unhappy start, Emily faces her new life bravely and soon starts to settle in at New Moon. She loves writing, especially poetry – although her passion gets her into trouble sometimes . . .

Emily was lost to her world – so lost that she did not know the geography class had scattered to their respective seats and that Miss Brownell, catching sight of Emily's entranced gaze skywards as she searched for a rhyme, was stepping softly towards her. Ilse was drawing a picture on her slate and did not see her or she would have warned Emily. The latter suddenly felt her slate drawn out of her hand and heard Miss Brownell saying, 'I suppose you have finished those sums, Emily?'

Emily had not finished even one sum – she had only covered her slate with verses – verses that Miss Brownell must not see – *must not* see! Emily sprang to her feet and clutched wildly after her slate. But Miss Brownell, with a smile of malicious enjoyment on her thin lips, held it beyond her reach.

'What is this? It does not look – exactly – like fractions. "Lines on the View – v-e-w – from the Window of Blair Water School." Really, children, we seem to have a budding poet among us.'

The words were harmless enough, but – oh, the hateful sneer that ran through the tone – the contempt, the mockery that was in it! It seared Emily's soul like a whiplash. Nothing was more terrible to her than the thought of having her beloved 'poems' read by stranger eyes – cold, unsympathetic, derisive, stranger eyes.

'Please – please, Miss Brownell,' she stammered miserably, 'don't read it – I'll rub it off – I'll do my sums right away. Only please don't read it. It – it isn't anything.'

Miss Brownell laughed cruelly.

'You are too modest, Emily. It is a whole slateful of – *poetry* – think of that, children – *poetry*. We have a pupil in this school who can write – *poetry*. And she does not want us to read this – *poetry*. I am afraid Emily is selfish. I am sure we should all enjoy this – *poetry*.'

Emily cringed every time Miss Brownell said '*poetry*' with that jeering emphasis and that hateful pause before it. Many of the children giggled, partly because they enjoyed seeing a 'Murray of New Moon' grilled, partly because they realised that Miss Brownell expected them to giggle. Rhoda Stuart giggled louder than anyone else; but Jennie Strang, who had tormented Emily on her first day at school, refused to giggle and scowled blackly at Miss Brownell instead.

Miss Brownell held up the slate and read Emily's poem aloud, in a sing-song nasal voice, with absurd intonations and gestures that made it seem a very ridiculous thing. The lines Emily had thought the finest seemed the most ridiculous. The other pupils laughed more than ever and Emily felt that the bitterness of the moment could never go out of her heart. The little fancies that had been so beautiful when they came to her as she wrote were shattered and bruised now, like torn and mangled butterflies. 'Vistas in some fairy dream,' chanted Miss Brownell, shutting her eyes and wagging her head from side to side. The giggles became shouts of laughter.

Oh, thought Emily, clenching her hands, *I wish – I wish the bears that ate the naughty children in the Bible would come and eat* you.

There were no nice, retributive bears in the school bush, however, and Miss Brownell read the whole 'poem' through. She was enjoying herself hugely. To ridicule a pupil always gave her pleasure and when that pupil was Emily of New Moon, in whose heart and soul she had always sensed something fundamentally different from her own, the pleasure was exquisite.

When she reached the end she handed the slate back to the crimson-cheeked Emily.

'Take your – *poetry*, Emily,' she said.

Emily snatched the slate. No slate 'rag' was handy but Emily gave the palm of her hand a fierce lick and one side of the slate was wiped off. Another lick – and the rest of the poem went. It had been disgraced – degraded – it must be blotted out of existence. To the end of her life Emily never forgot the pain and humiliation of that experience.

Miss Brownell laughed again.

'What a pity to obliterate such – *poetry*, Emily,' she said. 'Suppose you do those sums now. They are not – *poetry*, but I am in this school to teach arithmetic and I am not here to teach the art of writing – *poetry*. Go to your own seat. Yes, Rhoda?'

For Rhoda Stuart was holding up her hand and snapping her fingers.

'Please, Miss Brownell,' she said, with distinct triumph in her tones, 'Emily Starr has a whole bunch of poetry in her desk. She was reading it to Ilse Burnley this morning while you thought they were learning history.'

Perry Miller turned around and a delightful missile, compounded of chewed paper and known as a 'spit pill', flew across the room and struck Rhoda squarely in the face. But Miss Brownell was already at Emily's desk, having reached it one jump before Emily herself.

'Don't touch them – you have no *right*!' gasped Emily frantically.

But Miss Brownell had the 'bunch of poetry' in her hands. She turned and walked up to the platform. Emily followed. Those poems were very dear to her. She had composed them during the various stormy recesses when it had been impossible to play out of doors and written them down on disreputable scraps of paper borrowed from her mates. She had meant to take them home that very evening and copy them on letter-bills. And now this horrible woman was going to read them to the whole jeering, giggling school.

But Miss Brownell realised that the time was too short for that. She had to content herself with reading over the titles, with some appropriate comments.

Meanwhile Perry Miller was relieving his feelings by

bombarding Rhoda Stuart with spit pills, so craftily timed that Rhoda had no idea from what quarter of the room they were coming and so could not 'tell' on anyone. They greatly interfered with her enjoyment of Emily's scrape, however. As for Teddy Kent, who did not wage war with spit pills but preferred subtler methods of revenge, he was busy drawing something on a sheet of paper. Rhoda found the sheet on her desk the next morning; on it was depicted a small, scrawny monkey, hanging by its tail from a branch; and the face of the monkey was as the face of Rhoda Stuart. Whereat Rhoda Stuart waxed wrath, but for the sake of her own vanity tore the sketch to tatters and kept silence regarding it. She did not know that Teddy had made a similar sketch, with Miss Brownell figuring as a vampirish-looking bat, and thrust it into Emily's hand as they left school.

'"The Lost Dimond – a Romantic Tale",' read Miss Brownell. '"Lines on a Birch Tree" – looks to me more like lines on a very dirty piece of paper, Emily – "Lines Written on a Sundial in our Garden" – ditto – "Lines to my Favourite Cat" – another romantic *tail*, I presume – "Ode to Ilse" – "Thy neck is of a wondrous pearly sheen" – hardly that, I should say. Ilse's neck is very sunburned – "A Deskripshun of Our Parlour", "The Violets Spell" – I hope the violet *spells* better than you do, Emily –

"The Disappointed House" – "Lilies lifted up white cups, For the bees to *dr – r – i – i – nk*".'

'I didn't write it that way!' cried tortured Emily.

'"Lines to a Piece of Brokade in Aunt Laura's Burow Drawer", "Farewell on Leaving Home", "Lines to a Spruce Tree" – "It keeps off heat and sun and glare, 'Tis a goodly tree I ween" – are you quite sure that you know what "ween" means, Emily? – "Poem on Mr Tom Bennet's Field" – "Poem on the Vew from Aunt Elizabeth's Window" – you are strong on "v-e-w-s", Emily – "Epitaff on a Drowned Kitten", "Meditashuns at the Tomb of my Great-Great-Grandmother" – poor lady – "To my Northern Birds" – "Lines Composed on the Bank of Blair Water Gazing at the Stars" – hmm – hmm – "Crusted with uncounted gems, Those stars so distant, cold and true". Don't try to pass those lines off as your own, Emily. You couldn't have written them.'

'I did – I did!' Emily was white with a sense of outrage. 'And I've written lots far better.'

Miss Brownell suddenly crumpled the ragged little papers up in her hand.

'We have wasted enough time over this trash,' she said. 'Go to your seat, Emily.'

She moved towards the stove. For a moment Emily did not realise her purpose. Then, as Miss Brownell opened the stove door, Emily understood and bounded forward. She caught at the papers and tore them from Miss Brownell's hand before the latter could tighten her grasp.

'You *shall not* burn them – you shall not have them,' gasped Emily. She crammed the poems into the pocket of her 'baby apron' and faced Miss Brownell in a kind of calm rage. The Murray look was on her face – and although Miss Brownell was not so violently affected by it as Aunt Elizabeth had been, it nevertheless gave her an unpleasant sensation, as of having roused forces with which she dared not tamper further. This tormented child looked quite capable of flying at her, tooth and claw.

'Give me those papers, Emily,' – but she said it rather uncertainly.

'I will not,' said Emily stormily. 'They are mine. You have no right to them. I wrote them at recesses – I didn't break any rules. You' – Emily looked defiantly into Miss Brownell's cold eyes – 'you are an unjust, tyrannical *person*.'

Miss Brownell turned to her desk.

'I am coming up to New Moon tonight to tell your Aunt Elizabeth of this,' she said.

Emily was at first too much excited over saving her precious poetry to pay much heed to this threat. But as her excitement ebbed cold dread flowed in. She knew she had an unpleasant time ahead of her. But at all events they should not get her poems – not one of them, no matter what they did to *her*. As soon as she got home from school she flew to the garret and secreted them on the shelf of the old sofa.

She wanted terribly to cry but she would not. Miss Brownell was coming and Miss Brownell should *not* see her with red eyes. But her heart burned within her. Some sacred temple of her being had been desecrated and shamed. And more was yet to come, she felt wretchedly sure. Aunt Elizabeth was certain to side with Miss Brownell. Emily shrank from the impending ordeal with all the dread of a sensitive, fine-strung nature facing humiliation. She would not have been afraid of justice; but she knew at the bar of Aunt Elizabeth and Miss Brownell she would not have justice.

And I can't write Father about it, she thought, her little breast heaving. The shame of it all was too deep and intimate to be written out, and so she could find no relief for her pain.

They did not have supper at New Moon in winter time until Cousin Jimmy had finished his chores and was ready to stay in for the night. So Emily was left undisturbed in the garret.

From the dormer window she looked down on a dreamland scene that would ordinarily have delighted her. There was a red sunset behind the white, distant hills, shining through the dark trees like a great fire; there was a delicate blue tracery of bare branch shadows all over the crusted garden; there was a pale, ethereal alpen-glow all over the south-eastern sky; and presently there was a little, lovely new moon in the silvery arch over Lofty John's bush. But Emily found no pleasure in any of them.

Presently she saw Miss Brownell coming up the lane, under the white arms of the birches, with her mannish stride.

'If my father was alive,' said Emily, looking down at her, 'you would go away from this place with a flea in your ear.'

The minutes passed, each seeming very long to Emily. At last Aunt Laura came up.

'Your Aunt Elizabeth wants you to come down to the kitchen, Emily.'

Aunt Laura's voice was kind and sad. Emily fought down a sob. She hated to have Aunt Laura think she had been naughty, but she could not trust herself to explain. Aunt Laura would sympathise and sympathy would break her down. She went silently down the two long flights of stairs before Aunt Laura and out to the kitchen.

The supper table was set and the candles were lit. The

big black-raftered kitchen looked spookish and weird, as it always did by candlelight. Aunt Elizabeth sat rigidly by the table and her face was very hard. Miss Brownell sat in the rocking chair, her pale eyes glittering with triumphant malice. There seemed something baleful and poisonous in her very glance. Also her nose was very red – which did not add to her charm.

Cousin Jimmy, in his grey jumper, was perched on the edge of the woodbox, whistling at the ceiling, and looking more gnome-like than ever. Perry was nowhere to be seen. Emily was sorry for this. The presence of Perry, who was on her side, would have been a great moral support.

'I am sorry to say, Emily, that I have been hearing some very bad things about your behaviour in school today,' said Aunt Elizabeth.

'No, I don't think you are sorry,' said Emily, gravely.

Now that the crisis had come she found herself able to confront it coolly – nay, more, to take a curious interest in it under all her secret fear and shame, as if some part of her had detached itself from the rest and was interestedly absorbing impressions and analysing motives and describing settings. She felt that when she wrote about this scene later on she must not forget to describe the odd shadows the candle under Aunt Elizabeth's nose cast upward on her face, producing a rather skeletonic effect. As for Miss Brownell, could *she* ever have been a baby – a dimpled, fat, laughing baby? The thing was unbelievable.

'Don't speak impertinently to *me*,' said Aunt Elizabeth.

'You see,' said Miss Brownell, significantly.

'I don't mean to be impertinent, but you are *not* sorry,' persisted Emily. 'You are angry because you think I have disgraced New Moon, but you are a little glad that you have got someone to agree with you that I'm bad.'

'What a *grateful* child,' said Miss Brownell – flashing her eyes up at the ceiling – where they encountered a surprising sight. Perry Miller's head – and no more of him – was stuck down out of the 'black hole' and on Perry Miller's upside-down face was a most disrespectful and impish grimace. Face and head disappeared in a flash, leaving Miss Brownell staring foolishly at the ceiling.

'You have been behaving disgracefully in school,' said Aunt Elizabeth, who had not seen this byplay. 'I am ashamed of you.'

'It was not as bad as that, Aunt Elizabeth,' said Emily steadily. 'You see, it was this way—'

'I don't want to hear anything more about it,' said Aunt Elizabeth.

'But you must,' cried Emily. 'It isn't fair to listen

only to *her* side. I was a little bad – but not so bad as she says—'

'Not another word! I have heard the whole story,' said Aunt Elizabeth grimly.

'You heard a pack of lies,' said Perry, suddenly sticking his head down through the black hole again.

Everybody jumped – even Aunt Elizabeth, who at once became angrier than ever because she had jumped.

'Perry Miller, come down out of that loft instantly!' she commanded.

'Can't,' said Perry laconically.

'At once, I say!'

'Can't,' repeated Perry, winking audaciously at Miss Brownell.

'Perry Miller, come down! I *will* be obeyed. I am mistress here *yet*.'

'Oh, all right,' said Perry cheerfully. 'If I must.'

He swung himself down until his toes touched the ladder. Aunt Laura gave a little shriek. Everybody also seemed to be stricken dumb.

'I've just got my wet duds off,' Perry was saying cheerfully, waving his legs about to get a foothold on the ladder while he hung to the sides of the black hole with his elbows. 'Fell into the brook when I was watering the cows. Was going to put on dry ones – but just as you say—'

'Jimmy,' implored poor Elizabeth Murray, surrendering at discretion. *She* could not cope with the situation.

'Perry, get back into that loft and get your clothes on this minute!' ordered Cousin Jimmy.

The bare legs shot up and disappeared. There was a chuckle as mirthful and malicious as an owl's beyond the black hole. Aunt Elizabeth gave a convulsive gasp of relief and turned to Emily. She was determined to regain ascendancy and Emily must be thoroughly humbled.

'Emily, kneel down here before Miss Brownell and ask her pardon for your conduct today,' she said.

Into Emily's pale cheek came a scarlet protest. She could not do this – she would ask pardon of Miss Brownell but not on her knees. To kneel to this cruel woman who had hurt her so – she could not – would not do it. Her whole nature rose up in protest against such a humiliation.

'Kneel down,' repeated Aunt Elizabeth.

Miss Brownell looked pleased and expectant. It would be very satisfying to see this child who had defied her kneeling before her as a penitent. Never again, Miss Brownell felt, would Emily be able to look levelly at her with those dauntless eyes that bespoke a soul untameable and free, no matter what punishment might be inflicted upon body or mind. The memory of this moment would always be with Emily – she could never forget that she had knelt in abasement. Emily felt this as clearly as Miss Brownell did and remained stubbornly on her feet.

'Aunt Elizabeth, *please* let me tell my side of the story,' she pleaded.

'I have heard all I wish to hear of the matter. You will do as I say, Emily, or you will be outcast in this house until you do. No one will talk to you – play with you – eat with you – have anything to do with you until you have obeyed me.'

Emily shuddered. *That* was a punishment she could not face. To be cut off from her world – she knew it would bring her to terms before long. She might as well yield at once – but, ah, the bitterness, the shame of it!

'A human being should not kneel to anyone but God,' said Cousin Jimmy, unexpectedly, still staring at the ceiling.

A sudden strange change came over Elizabeth Murray's proud, angry face. She stood very still, looking at Cousin Jimmy – stood so long that Miss Brownell made a motion of petulant impatience.

'Emily,' said Aunt Elizabeth in a different tone. 'I was wrong – I shall not ask you to kneel. But you must apologise to your teacher – and I shall punish you later on.'

Emily put her hands behind her and looked straight into Miss Brownell's eyes again.

'I am sorry for anything I did today that was wrong,' she said, 'and I ask your pardon for it.'

Miss Brownell got on her feet. She felt herself cheated of a legitimate triumph. Whatever Emily's punishment would be she would not have the satisfaction of seeing it. She could have shaken Jimmy Murray with a right good will. But it would hardly do to show all she felt. Elizabeth Murray was not a trustee but she was the heaviest ratepayer in New Moon and had great influence with the School Board.

'I shall excuse your conduct if you behave yourself in future, Emily,' she said coldly. '*I* feel that I have only done my duty in putting the matter before your aunt. No, thank you, Miss Murray, I cannot stay to supper – I want to get home before it is too dark.'

'God speed all travellers,' said Perry cheerfully, climbing down his ladder – this time with his clothes on.

Aunt Elizabeth ignored him – she was not going to have a scene with a hired boy before Miss Brownell. The latter switched herself out and Aunt Elizabeth looked at Emily.

'You will eat your supper alone tonight, Emily, in the pantry – you will have bread and milk only. And you will not speak one word to anyone until tomorrow morning.'

'But you won't forbid me to think?' said Emily anxiously.

Aunt Elizabeth made no reply but sat haughtily down at the supper table. Emily went into the pantry and ate her bread and milk, with the odour of delicious sausages the others were eating for savour. Emily liked sausages, and New Moon sausages were the last word in sausages. Elizabeth Burnley had brought the recipe out from the Old Country and its secret was carefully guarded. And Emily was hungry. But she had escaped the unbearable, and things might be worse. It suddenly occurred to her that she would write an epic poem in imitation of *The Lay of the Last Minstrel*. Cousin Jimmy had read *The Lay* to her last Saturday. She would begin the first canto right off. When Laura Murray came into the pantry, Emily, her bread and milk only half eaten, was leaning her elbows on the dresser, gazing into space, with faintly moving lips and the light that never was on land or sea in her young eyes. Even the aroma of sausages was forgotten – was she not drinking from a fount of Castaly?

The WISE PRINCESS

Mary de Morgan

This fairy tale appears in a book called The Necklace of Princess Fiorimonde and Other Stories. *The author Mary de Morgan was a member of a women's suffragist group called the Women's Franchise League, who campaigned for women to have the right to vote, and she also worked at a school for girls. Her stories are often about girls and women who are brave and clever – just like this one.*

Once upon a time lived a king whose wife was dead and who had one little daughter who was named Fernanda. She was very good and pretty, but when she was a child she vexed all her ladies by asking them questions about everything she saw.

'Your Highness should not wish to know too much,' they told her, whereat Princess Fernanda threw up her little head, and said, 'I want to know everything.'

As she grew up she had masters and mistresses

to teach her, and learnt every language and every science; but still she said, 'It is not enough; I want to know more.'

In a deep cave underground there lived an old Wizard who was so wise that his face was well-nigh black with wrinkles, and his long white beard flowed to his feet. He knew all sorts of magic, and every day and night sat poring over his books till now there seemed to be nothing left for him to learn.

One night after every one was asleep, Princess Fernanda rose and slipped softly down the stairs and out of the palace unheard by anyone, and stole away to the Wizard's cave.

The old man was sitting on his low stool reading out of an immense book by a dim green light, but he raised his eyes as the princess entered at the low doorway, and looked at her. She wore a blue and silver robe, but her bright hair was unbound, and fell in ripples to her waist.

'Who are you, and what do you want with me?' he asked shortly.

'I am the Princess Fernanda,' she said, 'and I wish to be your pupil. Teach me all you know.'

'Why do you wish for that?' said the Wizard. 'You will not be better or happier for it.'

'I am not happy now,' said the princess, sighing

wearily. 'Teach me and you shall find me an apt pupil, and I will pay you with gold.'

'I will not have your gold,' said the Wizard, 'but come to me every night at this hour, and in three years you shall know all I do.'

So every night the princess went down to the Wizard's cave while all the court were sleeping. And the people wondered at her more and more, and said, 'How much she knows! How wise she is!'

When the three years had gone by the Wizard said to her, 'Go! I can teach you no more now. You are as wise as I.' Then the princess thanked him and went back to her father's palace.

She was very wise. She knew the languages of all animals. The fishes came from the deep at her call, and the birds from the trees. She could tell when the winds would rise, and when the sea would be still. She could have turned her enemies to stone, or given untold wealth to her friends. But for all that, when she smiled, her lips were very sad, and her eyes were always full of care. She said she was weary, and her father thought she was sick, and would have sent for the physicians, but she stopped him.

'How should physicians help me, my father,' she said, 'seeing that I know more than they?'

One night, a year after she had taken her last lesson

from the Wizard, she arose and returned to his cave, and he raised his eyes and saw her standing before him as formerly.

'What do you want?' he said. 'I have taught you all I know.'

'You have taught me much,' she said, falling on her knees beside him, 'yet I am ignorant of one thing – teach me that also – *how to be happy*.'

'Nay,' said the Wizard with a very mournful smile; 'I cannot teach you that, for I do not know it myself. Go and ask it of them who know and are wiser than I.'

Then the princess left the cave and wandered down to the seashore. All that night she spent sitting on a rock that jutted out into the sea, watching the wild sky and the moon coming and going behind the clouds. The sea dashed up around her, and the wind blew, but she did not fear them, and when the sun rose the waters were still and the wind fell. A skylark rose from the fields and flew straight up to heaven, singing as though his heart would burst with pure joy.

'Surely that bird is happy,' said the princess to herself; and she called it in its own tongue.

'Why do you sing?' she asked.

'I sing because I am so happy,' answered the lark.

'And why are you so happy?' asked the princess.

'So happy?' said the lark. 'God is so good. The sky is

so blue, and the fields are so green. Is that not enough to make me happy?'

'Teach me, then, that I may be happy too,' said Princess Fernanda.

'I cannot,' said the lark; 'I don't know how to teach;' and then he rose, singing, into the blue overhead, and Princess Fernanda sighed and turned back towards the palace.

Outside her door she met her little lapdog, who barked and jumped for joy on seeing her.

'Little dog,' she said; 'poor little dog, are you so glad to see me? Why are you so happy?'

'Why am I so happy?' said the little dog, surprised. 'I have plenty to eat, and a soft cushion to rest upon, and you to caress me. Is not it enough to make me happy?'

'It is not enough for me,' said the princess, sighing; but the little dog only wagged his tail and licked her hand.

Inside her room was the princess's favourite little maid Doris, folding up her dresses.

'Doris,' she said, 'you look very merry. Why are you so happy?'

'Please Your Royal Highness, I am going to the fair,' answered Doris, 'and Luke is to meet me there; only,' she added, pouting a little, 'I wish I had a pretty new hat to wear with my new dress.'

'Then you are not perfectly happy, so you cannot teach me,' said Princess Fernanda, and then she sighed again.

In the evening at sunset she arose, and went out into the village, and at the door of the first cottage to which she came, sat a woman nursing a baby, and hushing it to sleep. The baby was fat and rosy, and the mother looked down at it proudly.

The princess stopped, and spoke to her.

'You have a fine little child there,' she said. 'Surely you must be very happy.'

The woman smiled.

'Yes,' she said, 'so I am; only just now my goodman is out fishing, and as he's rather late, it makes me anxious.'

'Then you could not teach me,' said the princess, sighing to herself as she moved away. She wandered on till she came to a church, which she entered. All was still within, for the church was empty; but before the altar, on a splendid bier, lay the body of a young man, who had been killed in the war. He was dressed in his gay uniform, and his breast was covered with medals, and his sword lay beside him. He was shot through the heart, but his face was peaceful and his lips were smiling. The princess walked to his side, and looked at the quiet face. Then she stooped and kissed the cold forehead, and envied the soldier. 'If he could speak,' she said, 'he surely could teach me. No living mouth could ever smile like that.' Then she looked up and saw a white angel standing on the other side of the bier, and she knew it was Death.

'You have taught him,' she said, holding out her arms. 'Will you not teach me to smile like that?'

'Nay,' said Death, pointing to the medals on the dead man's breast, 'I taught him while he was doing his duty. I cannot teach you.' And so saying he vanished from her sight.

She went out from the church down to the seashore. There was a high sea, and a great wind, a little child had been playing on a row of rocks, and had slipped off them into the water, and was struggling among the waves, and would soon be drowned, for he was beyond his depth in the water.

When the princess saw him, she plunged into the water and swam to where the child was, and taking him in her arms, placed him safely on the rocks again, but the waves were so strong that she could scarcely keep above them. As she tried to seize the rocks, she saw Death coming over the water towards her, and she turned to meet him gladly.

'Now,' said he, clasping her in his arms, 'I will teach you all you want to know;' and he drew her under the water, and she died.

* * *

The king's servants found her lying on the shore, with her face white and her lips cold, but smiling as they had never smiled before, and her face was very calm. They carried her home, and she was laid out in great state, covered with gold and silver.

'She was so wise,' sobbed her little maid, as she placed flowers in the cold hand, 'she knew everything.'

'Not everything,' said the skylark from the window; 'for she asked me, ignorant though I am, to teach her how to be happy.'

'That was the one thing I could not teach her,' said the old Wizard, looking at the dead princess's face. 'Yet I think now she must be wiser than I, and have learnt that too. For see how she smiles.'

The SECRET GARDEN

Frances Hodgson Burnett

Mary Lennox grows up in India, where her rich parents leave her to be cared for by servants. Because she is given everything she could want – except for love – she is spoilt, selfish and bad-tempered. When her parents and servants are killed by an outbreak of cholera Mary is sent to live with her uncle, Mr Craven, at his home in Yorkshire. Here she finds a secret garden hidden behind a locked door and begins learning how to grow things in it. With this, and the friendship of a friendly robin, the gardener Ben, her maid Martha and Martha's brother Dickon, Mary starts to become kinder and happier, and to think of others.

She was awakened in the night by the sound of rain beating with heavy drops against her window. It was pouring down in torrents and the wind was 'wuthering' round the corners and in the chimneys of the huge old house. Mary sat up in bed and felt miserable and angry.

'The rain is as contrary as I ever was,' she said. 'It came because it knew I did not want it.'

She threw herself back on her pillow and buried her face. She did not cry, but she lay and hated the sound of the heavily beating rain, she hated the wind and its 'wuthering'. She could not go to sleep again. The mournful sound kept her awake because she felt mournful herself. If she had felt happy it would probably have lulled her to sleep. How it 'wuthered' and how the big raindrops poured down and beat against the pane!

'It sounds just like a person lost on the moor and wandering on and on crying,' she said.

She had been lying awake turning from side to side for about an hour, when suddenly something made her sit up in bed and turn her head towards the door listening. She listened and she listened.

'It isn't the wind now,' she said in a loud whisper. 'That isn't the wind. It is different. It is that crying I heard before.'

The door of her room was ajar and the sound came down the corridor, a far-off faint sound of fretful crying. She listened for a few minutes and each minute she became more and more sure. She felt as if she must find out what it was. It seemed even stranger than the secret garden and the buried key. Perhaps the fact that she was in a rebellious mood made her bold. She put her foot out of bed and stood on the floor.

'I am going to find out what it is,' she said. 'Everybody is in bed and I don't care about Mrs Medlock – I don't care!'

There was a candle by her bedside and she took it up and went softly out of the room. The corridor looked very long and dark, but she was too excited to mind that. She thought she remembered the corners she must turn to find the short corridor with the door covered with tapestry – the one Mrs Medlock had come through the day she lost herself. The sound had come up that passage. So she went on with her dim light, almost feeling her way, her heart beating so loud that she fancied she could hear it. The far-off faint crying went on and led her. Sometimes it stopped for a moment or so and then began again. Was this the right corner to turn? She stopped and thought. Yes it was. Down this passage and then to the left, and then up two broad steps, and then to the right again. Yes, there was the tapestry door.

She pushed it open very gently and closed it behind her, and she stood in the corridor and could hear the crying quite plainly, though it was not loud. It was on the other side of the wall at her left and a few yards further on there was a door. She could see a glimmer of light coming from beneath it. The Someone was crying in that room, and it was quite a young Someone.

So she walked to the door and pushed it open, and there she was standing in the room!

It was a big room with ancient, handsome furniture in it. There was a low fire glowing faintly on the hearth and a night light burning by the side of a carved four-posted bed hung with brocade, and on the bed was lying a boy, crying fretfully.

Mary wondered if she was in a real place or if she had fallen asleep again and was dreaming without knowing it.

The boy had a sharp, delicate face the colour of ivory and he seemed to have eyes too big for it. He had also a lot of hair which tumbled over his forehead in heavy locks and made his thin face seem smaller. He looked like a boy who had been ill, but he was crying more as if he were tired and cross than as if he were in pain.

Mary stood near the door with her candle in her hand, holding her breath. Then she crept across the room, and as she drew nearer the light attracted the boy's attention and he turned his head on his pillow and stared at her, his grey eyes opening so wide that they seemed immense.

'Who are you?' he said at last in a half-frightened whisper. 'Are you a ghost?'

'No, I am not,' Mary answered, her own whisper sounding half frightened. 'Are you one?'

He stared and stared and stared. Mary could not help noticing what strange eyes he had. They were agate grey and they looked too big for his face because they had black lashes all round them.

'No,' he replied after waiting a moment or so. 'I am Colin.'

'Who is Colin?' she faltered.

'I am Colin Craven. Who are you?'

'I am Mary Lennox. Mr Craven is my uncle.'

'He is my father,' said the boy.

'Your father!' gasped Mary. 'No one ever told me he had a boy! Why didn't they?'

'Come here,' he said, still keeping his strange eyes fixed on her with an anxious expression.

She came close to the bed and he put out his hand and touched her.

'You are real, aren't you?' he said. 'I have such real dreams very often. You might be one of them.'

Mary had slipped on a woollen wrapper before she left her room and she put a piece of it between his fingers.

'Rub that and see how thick and warm it is,' she said. 'I will pinch you a little if you like, to show you how real I am. For a minute I thought you might be a dream too.'

'Where did you come from?' he asked.

'From my own room. The wind wuthered so I couldn't go to sleep and I heard someone crying and wanted to find out who it was. What were you crying for?'

'Because I couldn't go to sleep either and my head ached. Tell me your name again.'

'Mary Lennox. Did no one ever tell you I had come to live here?'

He was still fingering the fold of her wrapper, but he began to look a little more as if he believed in her reality.

'No,' he answered. 'They daren't.'

'Why?' asked Mary.

'Because I should have been afraid you would see me. I won't let people see me and talk me over.'

'Why?' Mary asked again, feeling more mystified every moment.

'Because I am like this always, ill and having to lie down. My father won't let people talk me over either. The servants are not allowed to speak about me. If I live I may be a hunchback, but I shan't live. My father hates to think I may be like him.'

'Oh, what a queer house this is!' Mary said. 'What a queer house! Everything is a kind of secret. Rooms are locked up and gardens are locked up – and you! Have you been locked up?'

'No. I stay in this room because I don't want to be moved out of it. It tires me too much.'

'Does your father come and see you?' Mary ventured.

'Sometimes. Generally when I am asleep. He doesn't want to see me.'

'Why?' Mary could not help asking again.

A sort of angry shadow passed over the boy's face.

'My mother died when I was born and it makes him wretched to look at me. He thinks I don't know, but I've heard people talking. He almost hates me.'

'He hates the garden, because she died,' said Mary half speaking to herself.

'What garden?' the boy asked.

'Oh! just – just a garden she used to like,' Mary stammered. 'Have you been here always?'

'Nearly always. Sometimes I have been taken to places at the seaside, but I won't stay because people stare at me. I used to wear an iron thing to keep my back straight, but a grand doctor came from London to see me and said it was stupid. He told them to take it off and keep me out in the fresh air. I hate fresh air and I don't want to go out.'

'I didn't when first I came here,' said Mary. 'Why do you keep looking at me like that?'

'Because of the dreams that are so real,' he answered rather fretfully. 'Sometimes when I open my eyes I don't believe I'm awake.'

'We're both awake,' said Mary. She glanced round the room with its high ceiling and shadowy corners and dim firelight. 'It looks quite like a dream, and it's the middle of the night, and everybody in the house is asleep – everybody but us. We are wide awake.'

'I don't want it to be a dream,' the boy said restlessly.

Mary thought of something all at once.

'If you don't like people to see you,' she began, 'do you want me to go away?'

He still held the fold of her wrapper and he gave it a little pull.

'No,' he said. 'I should be sure you were a dream if you went. If you are real, sit down on that big footstool and talk. I want to hear about you.'

Mary put down her candle on the table near the bed and sat down on the cushioned stool. She did not want to go away at all. She wanted to stay in the mysterious hidden-away room and talk to the mysterious boy.

The O'SULLIVAN TWINS at ST CLARE'S

Enid Blyton

Margery Fenworthy is a new girl at St Clare's. She is cross and rude, and the other girls don't understand why. They try to be friendly with her, but after she is especially rude to Miss Lewis, the history teacher, they all decide not to speak to her any more. When Erica makes it look as though Margery is playing mean pranks on Pat, Pat takes revenge by telling all the other girls Margery's secret – that she's been expelled from seven schools in the past. In the scene below Margery has overheard the girls gossiping about her. Can things ever be put right?

But one girl did not sleep that night. It was Margery. She lay in her dormitory, wide awake, thinking of what she had heard the girls say about her. Always, always, wherever she went, her secret was found out, and sooner or later she had to go. She didn't want to be at school. She didn't want to stay at home. She wished with all her might that she could go out into the world and find a job and earn her own living. It was dreadful going from school to school like this, getting worse every time!

The other girls slept soundly. Someone snored a little. Margery turned over to her left side and shut her eyes. If only she could go to sleep! If only she could stop thinking and thinking! What was going to happen tomorrow? Now that all the girls knew about her, things would be terrible.

She couldn't go home. She couldn't run away because she didn't have much money. There was simply nothing she could do but stay and be miserable – and when she was miserable she didn't care about anything in the world, and that made her rude and careless and sulky.

There isn't any way out for me, thought the girl. *There's simply nothing I can do. If only there was something – some way of escape from all this. But there isn't.*

She turned over on to her right side, and shut her eyes again. But in a moment they were wide open. It was impossible to go to sleep. She tried lying on her back, staring up into the dark. But that didn't make her sleepy either. She heard the school clock chime out. Eleven o'clock. Twelve o'clock. One o'clock. Two o'clock. Was there ever such a long night as this? At this rate the night would never, never be over.

'I'll get myself a drink of water,' said Margery, sitting

up. 'Maybe that will help me to go to sleep.'

She put on her dressing gown and slippers and found her torch. She switched it on. Its light showed her the sleeping forms of the other girls. No one stirred as she went down between the cubicles to the door.

She opened the door and went out into the passage. There was a bathroom not far off, with glasses. She went there and filled a glass with water. She took it to the window to drink it.

And it was while she was standing there, drinking the icy-cold water that she saw something that puzzled her. She forgot to finish the water, and set the glass down to peer out of the window.

The bathroom window faced the sickbay, which was a four-storey building, tall and rather narrow. It was in complete darkness except at one place.

A flickering light showed now and again from high up on the third storey. It came from a window there. Margery puzzled over it. She tried to think what it could be.

It looks like flickering firelight, she thought. *But who is sleeping on the third storey, I wonder? Wait a minute – surely that isn't the window of a bedroom? Surely it's the little window that gives light to the stairway that goes up to the top storey?*

She watched for a little while, trying to make certain. But in the darkness she couldn't be sure if it was the staircase window or a bedroom window. The light flickered on and on, exactly as if it were the glow of a bedroom fire, sometimes dancing up into flames and sometimes dying down.

'I'd better go back to bed,' said Margery to herself, shivering. 'It's probably the room where Erica is – and Matron has given her a fire in her bedroom for a treat. It's the flickering glow I can see.'

So back to bed she went – but she kept worrying a little about that curious light – and in the end she got out of bed once more to see if it was still there.

And this time, looking out of the bathroom window, she knew without any doubt what it was. It was Fire, Fire, Fire!

As soon as Margery saw the light for the second time, she gave a shout. The whole of the staircase window was lit up, and flames were shooting out of it!

'Fire!' yelled Margery, and darted off to Miss Roberts's room. She hammered on her door.

'Miss Roberts! Miss Roberts! Quick, come and look! The sickbay is on fire! Oh, quick!'

Miss Roberts woke with a jump. Her room faced on to the sickbay and she saw at once what Margery had just seen. Dragging on a dressing gown she ran to the door. Margery clutched hold of her.

'Miss Roberts! Shall I go across and see if Matron knows! I'm sure she doesn't!'

'Yes, run quickly!' said Miss Roberts. 'Don't wake any of the girls in this building, Margery – there's no need for them to know. Hurry now. I'll get Miss Theobald and we'll join you.'

Margery tore down the stairs and undid the side door. She raced across the piece of grass that separated the sickbay from the school. She hammered on the door there and shouted.

'Matron! Matron! Are you there?'

Matron was fast sleep on the second floor. She didn't wake. It was Queenie, one of the girls in bed with a chill who heard Margery shouting. She ran to the window and looked out.

'What is it, what is it?' she cried.

'The sickbay is on fire!' shouted Margery. 'Flames are coming out on the storey above you. Wake Matron!'

The girl darted into the Matron's room. She shook her hard, calling to her in fright. Matron woke up in a hurry and pulled on a coat.

Miss Theobald appeared with some of the other mistresses. Someone had telephoned for the fire engine.

Girls appeared from everywhere, in spite of mistresses' orders to go back to bed.

'Good gracious! Go back to bed when there's a

perfectly good fire on!' said Janet who, as usual, was eager to enjoy any experience that came her way. 'Golly, I've never seen a fire before! I'm going to enjoy this one. Nobody's in any danger!'

Girls swarmed all over the place. Matron tried to find the three who had had chills – Queenie, Rita and Erica. 'They mustn't stand about in this cold night air,' she said, very worried. 'Oh, there you are, Queenie. You are to go at once to the second-form dormitory and get into the first bed you see there. Is Rita with you – and where is Erica?'

'Rita's here,' said Queenie, 'and I think I saw Erica somewhere.'

'Well, find her and take her to bed at once,' ordered Matron. 'Where are the two nurses? Are they safe?'

Yes – they were safe. They were shivering in their coats nearby, watching the flames getting bigger and bigger.

'Matron, is everyone out of the sickbay?' asked Miss Theobald. 'Are you sure? All the girls? The nurses? Anyone else?'

'I've seen Queenie,' said Matron, 'and Rita – and Queenie said she saw Erica. Those are the only girls I had in. And the two nurses are out. They are over there.'

'Well, that's all right then,' said Miss Theobald in relief. 'Oh, I wish that fire engine would hurry up. I'm afraid the fourth storey will be completely burnt out.'

Queenie had not seen the right Erica. She had seen a girl called Erica, who was in the fourth form, and she had not known that Matron meant Erica of the second form. Erica was still in the sickbay.

No one knew this at all until suddenly Mam'zelle gave a scream and pointed with a trembling hand to the window of the top storey. 'Oh, *que c'est terrible*!' she cried. 'There is someone there!'

Poor Erica was at the window. She had been awakened by the smell of smoke, and had found her bedroom dark with the evil-smelling smoke that crept in under and around her door. Then she had heard the crackling of the flames.

In a terrible fright she had jumped up and tried to switch on her light. But nothing happened. The wires outside had been burnt and there was no light in her room. The girl felt for her torch and switched it on.

She ran to the door – but when she opened it a great roll of smoke unfolded itself and almost choked her. There was no way out down the staircase. It was in flames.

The fire had been started by an electric wire that had smouldered on the staircase, and had kindled the dry wood nearby. The staircase was old and soon burnt fiercely. There was no way out for Erica. She tried to run into the next room, from whose window there was a fire escape – but the smoke was so thick that it choked her and she had to run back into her own room. She shut the door and rushed to the window.

She threw it open, and thankfully breathed in the pure night air. 'Help!' she shouted in a weak voice. 'Help!'

No one heard her – but Mam'zelle saw her. Everyone looked up at Mam'zelle's shout, and a deep groan went up as they saw Erica at the window.

Miss Theobald went pale, and her heart beat fast. A girl up there! And the staircase burning!

'The fire engine isn't here,' she groaned. 'If only we had the fire engine to run up its ladder to that high window! Oh, when will it come?'

Someone had found the garden hose and was spraying water on the flames. But the force of water was feeble and made little difference to the fire. Erica shouted again.

'Help! Save me! Oh, save me!' She could see all the crowd of people below and she could not think why someone did not save her. She did not realise that the fire engine had not yet come, and that there was no ladder long enough to reach her.

'Where is the long garden ladder?' cried Margery suddenly, seeing a gardener nearby. 'Let's get it. Maybe we can send a rope up or something, even if the ladder isn't long enough!'

The men ran to get the longest ladder. They set it up against the wall and one of them ran up to the top. But it did not nearly reach to Erica's window.

'It's no good,' he said when he came down. 'It's impossible to reach. Where's that fire engine? It's a long time coming.'

'It's been called out to another fire,' said one of the mistresses, who had just heard the news. 'It's coming immediately.'

'Immediately!' cried Margery. 'Well, that's not soon enough! Erica will soon be trapped by the flames.'

Before anyone could stop her the girl threw off her dressing gown and rushed to the ladder. She was up it like a monkey, though Miss Theobald shouted to her to come back.

'You can't do anything, you silly girl!' cried the head mistress. 'Come down!'

Everyone watched Margery as she climbed to the very top of the ladder. The flames lit up the whole scene now, and the dark figure of the climbing girl could be clearly seen.

'What does she think she can do?' said Miss Roberts, in despair. 'She'll fall!'

But Margery had seen something that had given her an idea. To the right side of the ladder ran an iron pipe. Maybe she could swarm up that and get to Erica's

window. What she was going to do then she didn't know
– but she meant to do something!

She reached the top of the ladder. She put out a hand
and caught hold of the strong iron pipe hoping that it
was well nailed to the wall. Fortunately it was. Margery
swung herself from the ladder to the pipe, clutching
hold of it with her knees, and holding for dear life with
her hands.

And now all her training in the gym stood her in good
stead. All the scores of times she had climbed the ropes
there had strengthened her arms and legs, and made
them very steady and strong. It was far more difficult to
climb an unyielding pipe than to swarm up a pliant rope,
but Margery could do it. Up the pipe she went, pulling
herself by her arms, and clinging with her knees and
feet. Erica saw her coming.

'Oh, save me!' cried the girl, almost mad with fright.
Margery came up to the window. Now was the most
difficult part. She had to get safely from the pipe to the
windowsill.

'Erica! Hold on to something and give me a hand!'
yelled Margery, holding out her hand above the
windowsill. 'If you can give me a pull, I can get there.'

Erica gave her hand to Margery. She held on to a
heavy bookcase just inside the room, and Margery
swung herself strongly across to the sill from the pipe.

She put up a knee, grazing it badly on the sill, but she did not even feel the pain. In half a moment she was inside the room. Erica clung to her, weeping.

'Now don't be silly,' said Margery, shaking herself free and looking round the room, filled with dense black smoke. The flames were already just outside the door and the floor felt hot to her feet. 'There's no time to lose. Where's your bed?'

Erica pointed through the smoke to where her bed was. Margery ran to it, choking, and dragged the sheets and blankets off it. She ran back to the window, and leant her head outside to get some fresh air. Then she quickly tore the sheets in half.

'Oh, what are you doing?' cried Erica, thinking that Margery was quite mad. 'Take me out of the window with you!'

'I will in a moment,' said Margery, as she knotted the sheet strips firmly together. There were four long strips. Margery looked for something to tie one end to. As she looked the door fell in with a crash, and flames came into the room.

'Oh, quick, quick!' cried Erica. 'I shall jump!'

'No, you won't,' said Margery. 'You're going to be saved – and very quickly too. Look here – see how I've knotted this sheet – and tied it to the end of your bed. Help me to drag the bed to the window. That's right.'

Margery threw the other end of the sheet strips out of the window. The end almost reached the top of the ladder! There was no need to climb down the pipe this time!

Margery sat herself on the window-sill and made Erica come beside her. Below, the crowds of girls and mistresses were watching what was happening, hardly daring to breathe. One of the gardeners had gone up the ladder, hoping to help.

'Now do you think you can climb down this sheet rope I've made?' said Margery to the trembling Erica. 'Look – it should be quite easy.'

'Oh, no, I can't, I can't,' sobbed Erica, terrified. So Margery did a very brave thing. She took Erica on her back, and with the frightened girl clinging tightly to her, her arms holding fast, she began to climb down the sheet rope herself. Luckily the sheets were new and strong, and they held well.

Down went Margery and down, her arms almost pulled out of their sockets with Erica's weight. She felt with her feet for the ladder, and oh, how thankful she was when at last she felt the top rung, and a loud voice cried, 'Well done, miss! I've got you!'

The gardener at the top of the ladder reached for Erica, and took hold of her. He helped the weeping girl down, and Margery slid down the few remaining feet of the sheet rope.

What happened next nobody ever knew. It was likely that Margery was tired out with her amazing climb and equally amazing rescue, and that her feet slipped on the ladder – for somehow or other she lost her balance, and half slid, half fell down the ladder. She fell on the gardener, who helped to break her fall a little – but then she slid right off the ladder to the ground seven or eight feet below.

People rushed over to her – but Margery lay still. She had struck her head against something and was quite unconscious. Careful hands carried her into the big school just as the fire engine rumbled up with a great clangour of its big bell. In one minute strong jets of water were pouring on to the flames, and in five minutes the fire was under control.

But the top storey, as Miss Theobald had feared, was entirely burnt out. The room where Erica had been sleeping was a mass of black charred timbers.

The girls were ordered back to bed, and this time they went! But there was one name on everyone's lips that night – the name of a real heroine.

'Margery! Wasn't she wonderful! She saved Erica's life. Fancy her climbing that pipe like that. Let's pray she isn't much hurt. Margery! Well, wasn't she wonderful?'

The
LITTLE MERMAID

Hans Christian Andersen

You might know the story of The Little Mermaid *already from the Disney film, but the original fairy tale by Hans Christian Andersen is quite different. Here the little mermaid – who doesn't have a name – is the youngest of the Sea King's six daughters. When each mermaid turns fifteen they are allowed to swim to the surface to see the world above.*

None of them longed so much for her turn to come as the youngest, she who had the longest time to wait, and who was so quiet and thoughtful. Many nights she stood by the open window, looking up through the dark blue water, and watching the fish as they splashed about with their fins and tails. She could see the moon and stars shining faintly; but through the water they looked larger than they do to our eyes. When something like a black cloud passed between her and them, she knew that it was either a whale swimming over her head, or a ship full of human beings, who never imagined that a pretty little mermaid was standing beneath them, holding out her white hands towards the keel of their ship.

As soon as the eldest was fifteen, she was allowed to rise to the surface of the ocean. When she came back, she had hundreds of things to talk about; but the most beautiful, she said, was to lie in the moonlight, on a sandbank, in the quiet sea, near the coast, and to gaze on a large town nearby, where the lights were twinkling like hundreds of stars; to listen to the sounds of the music, the noise of carriages, and the voices of human beings, and then to hear the merry bells peal out from the church steeples; and because she could not go near to all those wonderful things, she longed for them more than ever. Oh, did not the youngest sister listen eagerly to all these descriptions? And afterwards, when she stood at the open window looking up through the dark blue water, she thought of the great city, with all its bustle and noise, and even fancied she could hear the sound of the church bells, down in the depths of the sea.

In another year the second sister received permission to rise to the surface of the water, and to swim about where she pleased. She rose just as the sun was setting, and this, she said, was the most beautiful sight of all. The whole sky looked like gold, while violet and rose-coloured clouds, which she could not describe, floated over her; and, still more rapidly than the clouds, flew a large flock of wild swans towards the setting sun, looking like a long white veil across the sea. She also swam towards the sun; but it sunk into the waves, and the rosy tints faded from the clouds and from the sea.

The third sister's turn followed; she was the boldest of them all, and she swam up a broad river that emptied itself into the sea. On the banks she saw green hills covered with beautiful vines; palaces and castles peeped out from amid the proud trees of the forest; she heard the birds singing, and the rays of the sun were so powerful that she was obliged often to dive down under the water to cool her burning face. In a narrow creek she found a whole troop of little human children, quite naked, and sporting about in the water; she wanted to play with them, but they fled in a great fright; and then a little black animal came to the water; it was a dog, but she did not know that, for she had never before seen one. This animal barked at her so terribly that she became frightened, and rushed back to the open sea. But she said she should never forget the beautiful forest, the green hills, and the pretty little children who could swim in the water, although they had not fish's tails.

The fourth sister was more timid; she remained in the midst of the sea, but she said it was quite as beautiful there as nearer the land. She could see for so many miles around her, and the sky above looked like a bell of glass. She had seen the ships, but at such a great distance that they looked like sea gulls. The dolphins sported in the waves, and the great whales spouted water from their nostrils till it seemed as if a hundred fountains were playing in every direction.

The fifth sister's birthday occurred in the winter; so when her turn came, she saw what the others had not seen the first time they went up. The sea looked quite green, and large icebergs were floating about, each like a pearl, she said, but larger and loftier than the churches built by men. They were of the most singular shapes, and glittered like diamonds. She had seated herself upon one of the largest, and let the wind play with her long hair, and she remarked that all the ships sailed by rapidly, and steered as far away as they could from the iceberg, as if they were afraid of it. Towards evening, as the sun went down, dark clouds covered the sky, the thunder rolled and the lightning flashed, and the red light glowed on the icebergs as they rocked and tossed on the heaving sea. On all the ships the sails were reefed with fear and trembling, while she sat calmly on the floating iceberg, watching the blue lightning, as it darted its forked flashes into the sea.

When first the sisters had permission to rise to the surface, they were each delighted with the new and beautiful sights they saw; but now, as grown-up girls, they could go when they pleased, and they had become indifferent about it. They wished themselves back again in the water, and after a month had passed they said it was much more beautiful down below, and pleasanter to be at home. Yet often, in the evening hours, the five sisters would twine their arms round each other, and rise to the surface, in a row. They had more beautiful voices than any human being could have; and before the approach of a storm, and when they expected a ship would be lost, they swam before the vessel, and sang sweetly of the delights to be found in the depths of the sea, and begging the sailors not to fear if they sank to the bottom. But the sailors could not understand the song, they took it for the howling of the storm. And these things were never to be beautiful for them; for if the ship sank, the men were drowned, and their dead bodies alone reached the palace of the Sea King.

When the sisters rose, arm in arm, through the water in this way, their youngest sister would stand quite alone, looking after them, ready to cry, only that the mermaids have no tears, and therefore they suffer more. 'Oh, were I but fifteen years old,' said she, 'I know that I shall love the world up there, and all the people who live in it.'

At last she reached her fifteenth year. 'Well, now, you

are grown up,' said the old dowager, her grandmother; 'so you must let me adorn you like your other sisters;' and she placed a wreath of white lilies in her hair, and every flower leaf was half a pearl. Then the old lady ordered eight great oysters to attach themselves to the tail of the princess to show her high rank.

'But they hurt me so,' said the little mermaid.

'Pride must suffer pain,' replied the old lady. Oh, how gladly she would have shaken off all this grandeur, and laid aside the heavy wreath! The red flowers in her own garden would have suited her much better, but she could not help herself: so she said, 'Farewell,' and rose as lightly as a bubble to the surface of the water. The sun had just set as she raised her head above the waves; but the clouds were tinted with crimson and gold, and through the glimmering twilight beamed the evening star in all its beauty. The sea was calm, and the air mild and fresh. A large ship, with three masts, lay becalmed on the water, with only one sail set; for not a breeze stiffed, and the sailors sat idle on deck or among the rigging. There was music and song on board; and, as darkness came on, a hundred coloured lanterns were lit, as if the flags of all nations waved in the air. The little mermaid swam close to the cabin windows; and now and then, as the waves lifted her up, she could look in through clear glass windowpanes, and see a number of well-dressed people within. Among them was a young prince, the most beautiful of all, with large black eyes; he was sixteen years of age, and his birthday was being kept with much rejoicing. The sailors were dancing on deck, but when the prince came out of the cabin, more than a hundred rockets rose in the air, making it as bright as day. The little mermaid was so startled that she dived underwater; and when she again stretched out her head, it appeared as if all the stars of heaven were falling around her, she had never seen such fireworks before. Great suns spurted fire about, splendid fireflies flew into the blue air, and everything was reflected in the clear, calm sea beneath. The ship itself was so brightly illuminated that all the people, and even the smallest rope, could be distinctly and plainly seen. And how handsome the young prince looked, as he pressed the hands of all present and smiled at them, while the music resounded through the clear night air.

It was very late; yet the little mermaid could not take her eyes from the ship, or from the beautiful prince. The coloured lanterns had been extinguished, no more rockets rose in the air, and the cannon had ceased firing; but the sea became restless, and a moaning, grumbling sound could be heard beneath the waves: still the little mermaid remained by the cabin window, rocking up and down on the water, which enabled her to look in. After a while, the sails were quickly unfurled, and the noble ship continued her passage; but soon the waves rose higher, heavy clouds darkened the sky, and lightning appeared in the distance. A dreadful storm was approaching; once more the sails were reefed, and the great ship pursued her flying course over the raging sea. The waves rose mountains high, as if they would have overtopped the mast; but the ship dived like a swan between them, and then rose again on their lofty, foaming crests. To the little mermaid this appeared pleasant sport; not so to the sailors. At length the ship groaned and creaked; the thick planks gave way under the lashing of the sea as it broke over the deck; the mainmast snapped asunder like a reed; the ship lay over on her side; and the water rushed in. The little mermaid now perceived that the crew were in danger; even she herself was obliged to be careful to avoid the beams and planks of the wreck which lay scattered on the water. At one moment it was so pitch dark that she could not see a single object, but a flash of lightning revealed the whole scene; she could see everyone who had been on board excepting the prince; when the ship parted, she had seen him sink into the deep waves, and she was glad, for she thought he would now be with her; and then she remembered that human beings could not live in the water, so that when he got down to her father's palace he would be quite dead. But he must not die. So she swam about among the beams and planks which strewed the surface of the sea, forgetting that they could crush her to pieces. Then she dived deeply under the dark waters, rising and falling with the waves, till at length she managed to reach the young prince, who was fast losing the power of swimming in that stormy sea. His limbs were failing him, his beautiful eyes were closed, and he would have died had not the little mermaid come to his assistance. She held his head above the water, and let the waves drift them where they would.

In the morning the storm had ceased; but of the ship not a single fragment could be seen. The sun rose up red and glowing from the water, and its beams brought back the hue of health to the prince's cheeks; but his eyes remained closed. The mermaid kissed his high, smooth forehead, and stroked back his wet hair; he seemed to her like the marble statue in her little garden, and she kissed him again, and wished that he might live. Presently they came in sight of land; she saw lofty blue mountains, on which the white snow rested as if a flock of swans were lying upon them. Near the coast were beautiful green forests, and close by stood a large building, whether a church or a convent she could not tell. Orange and citron trees grew in the garden, and before the door stood lofty palms. The sea here formed a little bay, in which the water was quite still, but very deep; so she swam with the handsome prince to the beach, which was covered with fine, white sand, and there she laid him in the warm sunshine, taking care to raise his head higher than his body. Then bells sounded in the large white building, and a number of young girls came into the garden. The little mermaid swam out further from the shore and placed herself between some high rocks that rose out of the water; then she covered her head and neck with the foam of the sea so that her little face might not be seen, and watched to see what would become of the poor prince. She did not wait long before she saw a young girl approach the spot where he lay. She seemed frightened at first, but only for a moment; then she fetched a number of people, and the mermaid saw that the prince came to life again, and smiled upon those who stood round him. But to her he sent no smile; he knew not that she had saved him.

ACKNOWLEDGEMENTS

Little Women by Louisa May Alcott, originally published in the USA in 1868

The Wonderful Wizard of Oz by L. Frank Baum, originally published in the USA in 1900

The Snow Queen by Hans Christian Andersen, originally published in *New Fairy Tales*, in Denmark in 1844

The Railway Children by E. Nesbit, originally published in Great Britain in 1906

Jane Eyre by Charlotte Brontë, originally published in Great Britain in 1847

Kate Crackernuts by Joseph Jacobs, originally published in *English Fairy Tales*, in Great Britain in 1890

Rebecca of Sunnybrook Farm by Kate Douglas Wiggin, originally published in the USA in 1903

FAVOURITE STORIES OF COURAGEOUS GIRLS

Five on a Treasure Island by Enid Blyton, originally published in Great Britain in 1942, © Hodder & Stoughton Limited

White Chrysanthemum by Yei Theodora Ozaki, originally published in *Japanese Fairy Tales*, in Great Britain in 1903

Understood Betsy by Dorothy Canfield Fisher, originally published in the USA in 1916

Alice's Adventures in Wonderland by Lewis Carroll, originally published in Great Britain in 1865

The Princess Who Loved Her Father Like Salt by Maive Stokes, originally published in *Indian Fairy Tales*, in India in 1879

A Little Princess by Frances Hodgson Burnett, originally published in the USA in 1905

The Phoenix and the Carpet by E. Nesbit, originally published in Great Britain in 1904

The Seven Ravens by The Brothers Grimm, originally published in Germany in 1812

Pollyanna by Eleanor H. Porter, originally published in the USA in 1913

Anne of Green Gables by L. M. Montgomery, originally published in Canada in 1908

The Pomegranate Seeds by Nathaniel Hawthorne, originally

ACKNOWLEDGEMENTS

published in *Tanglewood Tales for Boys and Girls*, in the USA in 1853

Wuthering Heights by Emily Brontë, originally published in Great Britain in 1847

Emily of New Moon by L. M. Montgomery, originally published in Canada in 1923

The Wise Princess by Mary de Morgan, originally published in *The Necklace of Princess Fiorimonde*, in Great Britain in 1880

The Secret Garden by Frances Hodgson Burnett, originally published in Great Britain and the USA in 1911

The O'Sullivan Twins at St Clare's by Enid Blyton, originally published in Great Britain in 1942, © Hodder & Stoughton Limited

The Little Mermaid by Hans Christian Andersen, originally published in *Fairy Tales Told for Children*, in Denmark in 1837

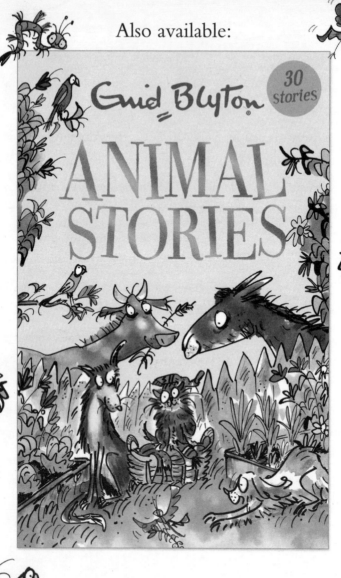

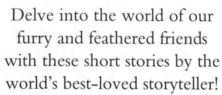

If you loved this collection, delve into another of these books, all starring bold and courageous girls . . .

Enter the Wundrous world of
Morrigan Crow in this magical series
by Jessica Townsend!

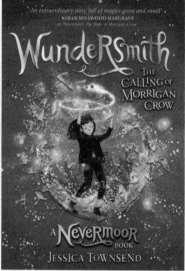

Join Justice Jones on her fearless search
for the truth in this murder mystery
unlike any other . . .

Set in the swamps of Louisiana,
read all about Eliza and Avery's heroic
adventure to save their community!